The hardmen were pinched in

They had been so consumed with charging Grimaldi that they had neglected to think a gunman could suddenly come roaring at them from the bar.

It proved to be their one big and very fatal mistake.

They tried to seek cover by their vehicles, but Grimaldi poured on the blistering autofire.

Bolan walked ahead, both weapons thundering, hammering out more slugs. The three remaining gunners never made their vehicles, nor did they ever know what hit them. One by one they cried out as bullets tore into them and flung them all over the lot.

Then one wounded gunman staggered to his feet, his chest soaked in crimson. He started to lift an Uzi submachine gun toward Bolan, snarling, "You're the goddamn bastard's been hitting us, ain't ya?"

One mighty thunderclap from the Executioner's Desert Eagle put the guy's question to eternal rest.

MACK BOLAN ®
The Executioner

DON PENDLETON'S
THE EXECUTIONER®
ROLLING DEATH

A GOLD EAGLE BOOK FROM
WORLDWIDE®

TORONTO • NEW YORK • LONDON
AMSTERDAM • PARIS • SYDNEY • HAMBURG
STOCKHOLM • ATHENS • TOKYO • MILAN
MADRID • WARSAW • BUDAPEST • AUCKLAND

First edition August 1999
ISBN 0-373-64248-2

Special thanks and acknowledgment to
Dan Schmidt for his contribution to this work.

ROLLING DEATH

No man is above the law and no man is below it; nor do we ask any man's permission when we require him to obey it. Obedience to the law is demanded as a right; not asked as a favor.

—Theodore Roosevelt

Everyone who doesn't obey the law is fair game. Drug lords, gunmen, even the chemists—all who are laboring to further poison America.

—Mack Bolan

THE
MACK BOLAN®
LEGEND

Nothing less than a war could have fashioned the destiny of the man called Mack Bolan. Bolan earned the Executioner title in the jungle hell of Vietnam.

But this soldier also wore another name—Sergeant Mercy. He was so tagged because of the compassion he showed to wounded comrades-in-arms and Vietnamese civilians.

Mack Bolan's second tour of duty ended prematurely when he was given emergency leave to return home and bury his family, victims of the Mob. Then he declared a one-man war against the Mafia.

He confronted the Families head-on from coast to coast, and soon a hope of victory began to appear. But Bolan had broken society's every rule. That same society started gunning for this elusive warrior—to no avail.

So Bolan was offered amnesty to work within the system against terrorism. This time, as an employee of Uncle Sam, Bolan became Colonel John Phoenix. With a command center at Stony Man Farm in Virginia, he and his new allies—Able Team and Phoenix Force—waged relentless war on a new adversary: the KGB.

But when his one true love, April Rose, died at the hands of the Soviet terror machine, Bolan severed all ties with Establishment authority.

Now, after a lengthy lone-wolf struggle and much soul-searching, the Executioner has agreed to enter an "arm's-length" alliance with his government once more, reserving the right to pursue personal missions in his Everlasting War.

1

The old Don of South Florida was lined up in the Executioner's deathsights. It would've been so easy. One gentle squeeze of the Remington 700 rifle's trigger, and the balding pate of Paul "Paolo" Tartaglia would've erupted in a sudden burst of brains in the crosshairs of Mack Bolan's custom-made Starlight scope.

Too easy. Not yet. Probably not even today.

No, Bolan intended to save Don Paolo to reel in all the fish, so no one could take his place. Today, tonight or tomorrow, there would be no escape for this new enemy of the Executioner.

Bolan shifted the aim of the sniper rifle. He drew a bead on one of Don Paolo's lieutenants, Vinnie Carmine, then adjusted the scope to frame the neatly trimmed jet black mane in the crosshairs. Yet another savage who had to wait.

The soldier continued his search through the scope. Decisions, decisions.

They were all gathering on the white sands of the Don's exclusive beachfront property in Miami Beach. He counted six soldiers standing guard along the seawall, a couple of them lounging and smoking around the palm trees that lined Collins Avenue.

There were two members of the Tartaglia organization the Executioner was particularly interested in. Right now, those men were stepping out of their vehicles. One lanky figure emerged from a black Porsche, and the other guy slid out of a red Jaguar. According to DEA intelligence, obtained by Hal Brognola, they were Marty Barikan and Stan Peterson, two of Tartaglia's main cocaine distributors in South Florida and points north and west. Barikan posed as real-estate investor while Peterson fronted as an accountant for all of the "legit" Tartaglia businesses.

The two distributors were decked out in loud Hawaiian shirts, silk slacks and Italian loafers. A lot of neck and wrist jewelry flashed from the street below. They were looking good, all right.

They were marked for extinction.

Bolan lowered the rifle, then picked up his high-powered field glasses. Before returning to his surveillance, the soldier gave his rooftop vantage a hard sweep.

Bolan was alone on the sprawling roof of the high-rise condo. The entire stretch north was choked with condominiums and hotels. Just south, he saw the square-mile clutter of the Art Deco District. Behind Bolan, the glittering skyline of Miami loomed, directly across Biscayne Bay where the rich jetted up and down in their pleasure craft. His position was above the top levels of the closest buildings to the action. Anyone would need binoculars to spot him.

During the day, Bolan had trailed Carmine to various Tartaglia businesses around the Miami area. Judging by the paranoia he had seen on the man's face, Bolan suspected something major was in the wings. But the Executioner had already caught rumblings from Brognola that the Tartaglia Family was looking to launch a major coup—one that would, allegedly, fatten their offshore bank accounts by billions of illicit dollars, or get funneled into another hotel or condominium.

But the facts were sketchy, since the intel had come via a DEA informant. It seemed the snitch was a former narcotics distributor of the Family but had fallen out of grace with the Don for skimming a brick here, a brick there. Now the guy was in hiding. Later, Bolan intended to round that snitch up and shake his tree. No doubt, the guy wanted a sweetheart deal to sing. All the snitch would get from Bolan might be life over certain death.

Right now, it was time to turn on the killing heat against the multibillion-dollar drug empire in South Florida. Business was still booming in Miami. In fact, Brognola had informed Bolan the modern-day alchemists were dumping more poison onto the shores of Florida than ever before.

Despite the fact that the people of Miami resented the stigma of being the drug capital of the country, cocaine was still king there. The drug trade had changed some over the past few years, of course. Before heading out from Washington, D.C., Bolan had gotten somewhat up-to-speed on the narcotics situation in the New York City of the south.

The traffickers, whether they were from the lower Americas or of Italian descent, had taken a pummeling in recent years. But the bottom line was they were still in business. Heat from the DEA, Coast Guard, Justice Department and other law-enforcement agencies had merely forced the traffickers to bury their business a little deeper underground. These days, they came out with college degrees and snapped up real-estate licenses. They were lawyers or they went into banking, while laundering the billions earned by the legions who poisoned America. They made offshore investments, or, as the Tartaglias had done, they built condos in the recent construction boom of Miami Beach. For years, the Tartaglias had done their best to go respectable. In fact, Don Paolo had been hard at work putting on a legitimate face for twenty years.

Everywhere Bolan dogged Vinnie Carmine during the day, he found the Family-owned businesses ranged from citrus and trucking to a chain of sports stores, restaurants, even a strip joint called Baby Doll Heaven. Every last one of them, Bolan knew, was a front. They either did their drug transactions from these so-called places of business, stored their loads, or laundered their money. Later, Bolan would learn more from a DEA contact Brognola had arranged for the soldier to meet. He needed the details about a growing link between the Tartaglia Family and the Cali Cartel.

South Florida had been long overdue for a visit by the Executioner.

Peering over the roof's edge, surveying the enemy

through the binoculars, Bolan waited while they did the handshakes and went through the roving paranoid search of their surroundings. Don Tartaglia was out of his lawn chair, puffing on his foot-long Havana cigar. He was a big man, a little paunchy around the middle, but broad-shouldered with some muscular definition still in his arms and chest. With a wave of his hand the Don sent his two playmates, a nubile blonde and a brunette, both in string bikinis, away with one of his soldiers.

Tucking the field glasses back in the large duffel bag, Bolan attached the sound suppressor to the Remington 700. He hunched, settling in the deep shadows behind the bank of air-conditioning units.

It was no accident he'd picked this rooftop as the point to launch this campaign against the Tartaglias. The Don spent two hours every evening, in the sand, right there.

The Family owned the building, and Bolan had taken a recently vacated suite, one floor beneath their penthouse. Brognola could work wonders when he saw the opportunity.

The Executioner snugged the rifle's stock against his shoulder. There was a hot breeze hitting his back, but the heat was always fierce that time of year in Miami. The soldier gauged the distance to the targets as roughly the length of a football field.

The sniper rifle had a range of 820 meters. In the hands of Mack Bolan, the Remington 700 was more than adequate. At that distance, shooting down with a breeze at his back, it would be a sure shot. Vipers all in a nest, stomped underfoot.

Bolan slipped his finger around the trigger and sighted through the scope.

Decision made.

LIFE WAS GOOD these days for Paul Tartaglia, and he intended to keep it that way.

Sandals on, he led his two distributors toward the surf. Puffing on his expensive Cuban cigar, he listened to the gentle lap of waves breaking on the beach. One of his soldiers trailed them, while the rest of his crew was near the seawall, keeping an eye on the street for any unmarked units. Dark shades on, Vince Morinelli was checking the nearly deserted beach, the bulge of a holstered side arm beneath his light windbreaker. Tartaglia saw nothing but a few dogs and a Frisbee flying disk thrower. Then he spotted two comely blondes, soaking up the last of the day's sunshine. They were catching a little more attention from Morinelli than the Don liked. But Tartaglia made a mental note to approach the beauties when his meet was over, offer them a drink, maybe more.

It was surely a beautiful time of day, Tartaglia decided. The sun was setting, throwing a reddish-gold light across the dark green waters of the Atlantic Ocean. Even the white sands were starting to cool off, no longer like hot coals under the feet. A good time of day to be alive, to reflect, to work on the future.

Turning his head a little, he looked north. For a moment, Tartaglia thought of his father and felt a stab of fierce gratitude. All he had, he owed to his father.

Vincenzo Tartaglia had come from Sicily a little more than a half-a-century ago with his young wife, and only the shirt on his back. From the old country he had re-established contacts among the founding Families in New York. Given his reputation as a man of honor who'd go the distance to prove his loyalty, he had eventually become a button man for one of the Families. He had been trusted, respected, nearly worshiped by all, friend or foe. Of course, back then, there were always the usual shooting wars, the power struggles, guys grabbing for more than their rightful share. Not Vincenzo Tartaglia. He knew how to make friends and take care of enemies. Don Paolo's father had survived all the interfamily battles of the forties and fifties, proving his merit as a man of respect. Eventually, the Five Families had gotten together and decided to carve up South Florida.

And Vincenzo Tartaglia was bestowed the honor to launch a number of businesses there. They ranged from gambling and loan sharking to escort services. Still, the old man never turned the megafortune New York had envisioned. No one ever got upset with Vincenzo for not handing Miami over to the Families on a gold platter. Vincenzo was his own man, and after all, special.

When the old man had died in the late sixties, young Paolo, the elder of two brothers, had inherited the kingdom. His father had done well enough, but Paul Tartaglia wanted to make his own mark in the world. Even back then he had seen the future. And it had been cocaine.

Right now the future was in trouble.

There were rumors and rumblings of informants in his organization everywhere he turned. In the old days, he did the muscle work himself, breaking a head, or killing a man if some guy weaseled or snitched. Then he got smart and left the bloodletting to his soldiers. Even smarter, he kept a good distance from the business of establishing and maintaining the distribution network. It was best to run so-called legitimate activities from an office in downtown Miami or out of his Palm Beach estate. Still, maybe broker a major deal once in a while just to stay sharp.

Of course, Don Paolo always had to deal with the Colombians. Even if tried, he couldn't tell a Medellín guy from a Cali punk. They were all cut from the same vicious cloth, cold-blooded killers who'd wipe out a guy's whole family just for chuckles. Where was the honor in that?

Still, they manufactured a product that reaped the Don a little over one billion dollars a year. Naturally, with that much money coming in or working for him in legitimate areas of business, there were always problems keeping the ship afloat. All it took was one guy going to the DEA to let his nightmare begin. Almost without exception, though, guys got busted because they had big mouths, usually bragging to some baby doll they wanted to impress. Or they got pulled over flying down the road with a nose full of powder, giving a cop more than enough probable cause to open up a trunk, thus finding serious sale weight. Those kind of guys Tartaglia always spotted from a mile away. Flash he didn't need because it drew attention. Let the Colombians and the blacks show off. He caught a glimpse of Barikan and Peterson, the shirts and jewelry nearly blinding him. It was something he needed to mention to them later.

However it was sliced, the rewards always outweighed the risks. If it wasn't for cocaine, he knew, Miami, all of South Florida, in fact, would need a government handout to stay alive. Anyway, he had cops and judges, even a couple of DEA guys in his pocket, so he kept his ears tuned to any developing situations.

But things were heating up. It was something he needed to address, but not now. There was no sense in dropping a hammer on his two main movers and shakers and have them sweating blood when a major deal was in the wings.

Tartaglia turned, smiling at the string of towering condos. "You know, gentlemen," he said, puffing lightly on his stogie, "life is sweet right now. It's taken a lot of work, but I've put a new face on Miami Beach. Used to be you saw them everywhere down here, with their walkers, oxygen masks and catheters. One goddamn giant geriatric funeral parlor. The stink of slow dying was all around, and you couldn't get away from it. Well, I changed it. We moved in, built half this town from the ground up again. We've got movie and rock stars and politicians in Miami Beach now. It's a beautiful thing.

These days, you got to look real hard to find some blue-haired bags, maybe playing bridge, hungry for that next social-security check.'' He snorted, then spoke with a voice of utter contempt. ''Old people have gotten as ugly as the blacks, acting like somebody owes them something. If I had my way, I'd round them all up, stuff their withered asses in an oven, catheters and all.''

Tartaglia saw them fidget a little. They knew he was headed somewhere but weren't sure of the point. ''Hell, just last night this hot-shit action movie hero, who wants to play a big-time crime boss in his next picture, was dripping schmooze all over me. Said he'd been dying to meet me for years. Bad choice of words, but this guy's a clown. He wouldn't know a real piece from a BB gun. He said he wanted to put a sympathetic touch to the character of this underworld figure. Imagine that. A sensitive politically correct Boss of Bosses.'' The Don chuckled, and Barikan and Peterson forced a laugh.

Don Paolo watched them shift around some more in the sand. ''My bigger point is I don't want to be like that guy on my worst day. Big celeb, all softened up by his own bloated ego while the sharks circle. Hell, I could've reached out and touched him right there, if you know what I mean. Still, things have been too damn good, too damn quiet for too long. We're getting soft, and we're not playboy movie stars. The sharks are always circling. Our people have been getting hit hard lately. Uncle Sam takes our boats, our cars, our businesses, leaving us groveling for enough chump change to get smokes and a bottle of whiskey. I'll die before I end up like that.''

The Don let the silence hang for a moment. ''The reason we're here is because you need to get those funds rounded up, ASAP.''

Peterson cleared his throat. ''Uh, sir, we're having some problems with New Orleans. They were hit by the DEA last week. What you just said happened. They snatched up everything, including bank accounts from the Bahamas to Switzerland. In a word, it's a fiasco.''

''Tell me something I don't know,'' Tartaglia growled. ''I read about it in the papers. What I need to know is, are we covered?''

''Books are in order,'' Peterson said. ''Accounts can't be traced here.''

''Your word's as good as gold,'' Don Paolo said, smiling. ''I just want to know if we can be ready to move on this new deal when I meet with them tomorrow.''

Barikan spoke up. ''It shouldn't be a problem. The funds are there. I just need to cover the tracks of one of my couriers. The man's reliable. We're just making sure it's safe for him to move.''

''Couple of suitcases full of cash, huh?'' Tartaglia frowned. ''That's not the usual, but they told me that's the way they want it, at least for the first time out.''

They all knew what was about to go down, how important it was everything went off without a hitch.

Recently, the Colombians had started growing poppies in the Andes Mountains. Heroin was fast becoming the latest rage in narcotics, a more mellow high in these stressful times. So a man had to adjust, change with the times. Bottom line, it sounded like there was as much, if not more money to be made in heroin than cocaine. All they had to do was set it up right, then find reliable wholesalers on the other end.

Tartaglia agreed their house was in order. Tonight's shipment was set to be moved by truck to Orlando. There, Peterson would store half of the one hundred keys in several hidden floor and wall compartments in his office until the situation in New Orleans was settled. Either way, Atlanta, Houston and L.A. were still dependable and eager to beef up their supplies of cocaine.

Don Paolo was feeling a little better about the future after talking with his two main distributors. It was good to have a face-to-face like this, once a week or so, to touch base, feel things out. He gazed out across the Atlantic Ocean one more time. He was silently acknowledging his gratitude to his father for making all of this possible, when something wet and hot was suddenly spattering his back and the side of his face. Instinctively, he already knew what was happening. Shock led to a moment's paralysis.

Fear tore through him. He felt his jaw muscles react, snapping off the end of the cigar in his clenched teeth. Tartaglia saw that the back of Peterson's head had exploded. Blood and brains were still flying through the air. The guy was still standing, teetering as his mutilated brain tried to register he was dead on his feet. Before it registered, Don Paolo witnessed Morinelli's face shatter into pulpy goo. His bodyguard hit the sand as if he'd been slammed in the face by a wrecking ball.

Tartaglia's soldiers raced down the beach, weapons drawn. But they were looking in the wrong direction. Whoever was hitting them wasn't planted in the sand, mint julep by his side. Hell, no. He or they were somewhere up on the rooftop of one of the condos. Tartaglia wanted to scream at them for spilling onto the beach like they were seizing Normandy when he knew the hitter wasn't anywhere within visible eyeshot.

Tartaglia bumped into Barikan, who was stumbling through the sand. The man was shrieking in his fear. In the next instant Don Paolo glimpsed the distributor's skull burst apart like a ripe melon.

IT WAS A MESSAGE, pure and simple. Three gentle squeezes of the trigger, and the Executioner sent three men toppling to the sand. The Family was in a panic. The Don was trying to gather himself, bolting across the beach for cover, but there was nothing except a palm tree. Bolan could imagine Tartaglia's terror.

The message to them was that they weren't untouchable.

Bolan shifted his aim. Two shots remained in the 5-shot magazine. He cocked the bolt action, drawing a bead on a guard flying toward the street. The gunman never looked up. By the time he figured out the attack was hitting them from above, Bolan had cored a 7.62 mm NATO slug through his face. Muzzling down at 850 meters per second, the sizzling lead tore through the hardman's forehead, the back of his skull evaporating in a pink halo.

Bolan drilled one more shot through the chest of another gunner. He sent him flying over the hood of the Porsche, a crimson trail streaking the black hood.

Time to go.

The soldier set down the rifle. He would leave everything right there. The weapons and gear were untraceable. On the way down, he'd attach a fake mustache and beard, and slip on the thick eyeglasses. Then he'd calmly exit through the condo lobby, never to return.

On the move for the rooftop door, Bolan checked his chronometer. He hadn't come to Miami alone. Right then, Special Agent Jack Griswald, aka Jack Grimaldi, was moving on a Tartaglia warehouse along the Miami River.

They'd deliver a one-two punch, rubbing salt into a wound the Executioner had just opened on South Florida's cocaine king.

2

Jack Grimaldi cut through the bottom of the chain-link fence with razor-sharp wire cutters. He'd already checked it with a soft toss of a soda can, just to make sure it wasn't electrified. No sign of cameras or motion detectors either. So far, so good.

But this was a place of "legitimate" business for the Tartaglia brothers, a citrus warehouse by the Miami River. Brognola's DEA source indicated they probably shipped more cocaine out of there than oranges or grapefruits.

At first glance, security seemed lax, but it made sense to Grimaldi. There was no point in upsetting Miami's finest and have them tear through the place because a stray vagrant or mongrel had wandered into the fence, and promptly been barbecued by accident.

They were, in fact, moving a shipment, Grimaldi saw, loading a dark blue van by the shipping door of the warehouse. Across a stretch of no-man's-land, he counted six men. Even at a distance he detected the bulge of holstered side arms beneath their sports coats or windbreakers. Then he caught a fleeting glimpse of a shadow in the doorway of the warehouse, toting an assault rifle. It looked like the intel was right. Couple the hardware with the grim paranoia that appeared as they constantly scanned the area, and Grimaldi knew he was stepping up to the plate, ninth inning, bases loaded. How much cocaine was being moved and to where, Grimaldi didn't know, but he cared.

He was there as part of a scorched-earth policy, to be inflicted on the Tartaglias and whomever else they did business with. Either together with the big guy, or working alone on separate initial phases of the campaign, Grimaldi wasn't about to let Mack Bolan down.

Crouched, an M-72 disposable rocket launcher slung around his shoulder, an Uzi submachine gun poised to fire if it suddenly went south on him, Stony Man Farm's ace pilot slid through the opening. Swiftly he crept behind a large trash bin at the edge of the lot.

Darkness was falling fast. Grimaldi set his sights on his prey. He briefly thought about Bolan, his long-time friend and ally. Brognola had laid the urgency on both men about this new and burgeoning flood of narcotics into South Florida. The traffickers were either hungrier than ever or something ominous was building. Two recent busts of Panamanian freighters off the coast of Florida had seen the DEA and Coast Guard seize more than fifteen tons of cocaine and two tons of heroin. Street informers and undercover narcotics officers had still witnessed a dramatic drop in prices despite these huge seizures. The reason was simple, Grimaldi knew. There was more cocaine being smuggled in, and out there on the city streets than ever.

So Brognola had sent in a two-man strike force. Rumor had it there was a new team of Cali traffickers in town, looking to set up shop. Word was they were looking to add heroin to the ocean of white poison they'd already flooded into America. Well, Grimaldi knew Mack Bolan would have something to say about that.

In fact, the war against the traffickers had already started. Brognola had moved fast on this one. Deep in the Everglades the Justice Man had worked his magic, setting up a temporary base of operations for them. At the base, Grimaldi knew they had two new "war toys" for this mission. The gunship was his personal vehicle to track, dog and eat up any enemy from above. And Bolan would use a custom-built war wagon for groundwork. Right then, the base was guarded by three men from Stony Man Farm.

First order of business, though, was to hit Tartaglia where it hurt the worst.

Maybe a million dollars' worth of misery.

Grimaldi gave the area a hard search. Other buildings cropped up in the distance, some with brightly lit lots, others dark and looking abandoned. The five-mile waterway of the Miami River had eleven bridges to let all manner of vessels to pass. Tugs, freighters, even yachts floated along the river at all hours of the night.

The pilot peered around the corner of the bin, waiting until it looked as if they had loaded the last of the wooden crates into the back of the van. Then he snapped the two concentric tubes together. Locked in place, he raised the sights on the launcher. The lone 66 mm HEAT missile inside the tube could penetrate over 300 mm of armor.

He was anxious to find out what it would do to mere metal.

Grimaldi triggered the warhead. Downrange, the men looked up, their natural fear and paranoia making them grab for hardware. The pilot caught a glimpse of the shock and terror in their eyes as the rocket sizzled on target. Impact came like a clap of thunder, and a roaring fireball incinerated the van. Bodies and body parts were thrown all over the lot. A chunk of fiery wreckage fell to the ground. In the firelight, Grimaldi saw several cocaine bricks hammer the concrete. When they burst, spewing white powder, it confirmed he'd just hit a grand slam.

The pilot started to retreat then he saw armed shadows surging down the weed-choked bank toward him. DEA was stenciled, white and bold, on their dark windbreakers.

Grimaldi shot his hands up. "Easy, fellas. I'm with the Justice Department."

They surrounded the pilot, assault rifles and pistols trained in rock-steady fists on his chest. Behind, Grimaldi glimpsed a gunman survivor, staggering to his feet, firing away with an assault rifle. But he went down hard in a quick burst of DEA autofire.

Grimaldi searched the grim faces surrounding him. This wasn't good. By pure accident, he had just stumbled across a major raid by the DEA and blown their ambitions of a big seizure all to hell.

A black giant with a shaved head approached Grimaldi. There was pure fire in his dark eyes. "You're going to have one hell of a time convincing me of that."

BABY DOLL HEAVEN was a gold mine of cocaine, fast money and hot women. It was the sweetest setup Ricky "The Blond Jet" Mathers could've ever dreamed possible. He smiled from behind his desk in the back office as he leaned back in the black leather, high-backed chair, smoothing his shoulder-length blond hair.

Twelve cameras monitored the floors, divided equally between the lower and upper levels. Twelve cameras was hardly enough to catch all the naked women out there. Mathers gave himself a squeeze, loving what he saw. Money, drugs and sex—was there anything more to life? Like the professional barracudas they all were, the girls worked the floor, stroking guys with a "maybe later, hon", table topping or lap dancing. Silently, Mathers urged his girls on. Shake it some more, pluck up those fives and tens. Ah, life was good.

He did a fat line of ninety percent Peruvian flake with a gold tube. While the sharp but sweet bite of the powder hit his brain, Mathers watched the two new girls on the floor. Both were blonde, young and working their way through college, or so the story went. He hadn't done the interview before they were hired, but he decided to introduce himself later as the manager and co-owner of the club.

He got up, went to the wet bar and built himself

a double Wild Turkey whiskey with a splash of ginger. It hadn't always been this good. The fact was, he'd been down on his luck up until six months ago.

He drank fast. The booze hitting his belly would help neutralize the intense rush of euphoria. Without a stiff drink, the chemically induced heaven of the coke would quickly threaten to turn to jitters. Sometimes even the onslaught of depression would wash over him within a few minutes after the first wave of shakes wore off. He hated to feel down.

He was alone in his office at the moment, and Mathers hated being alone. He always began to think about the past—the ghosts and failures of all that should have and could have happened.

He had been a professional football player, a two-time Pro Bowl wide receiver, praised and drooled on all over town. But his career of four years had been cut short when he'd violated the NFL's drug policy for the third time and was banned for life. Well, when he'd been catching touchdown passes and lighting up the reporters with his boyish good looks, wit and charm, he'd done the right thing for himself.

Yes, he knew there'd come a day when he had to quit or was forced into retirement. Back then everybody loved him, wanted to know him, wanted something from the fast as wind golden-haired Adonis of the league. A little toot here, handing out a decent cash loan there, but always to the right people—the grateful ones—and his tomorrow was set. When the time came, he'd called in the right markers.

One of those people had been the owner of Baby

Doll Heaven. His new partner, John Majors, had always been a football fanatic. It hadn't taken too much of the smile and quick wit before Mathers landed himself a position as co-owner. He was in, and knew full well the strip joint was owned by Mob boss Paul Tartaglia. Mathers had no problem with that. Give respect where respect was due.

He was a Baby Doll kind of guy, all right, part of the exclusive club, one of the beautiful people with a solid tomorrow. So he wasn't allowed access to the books, fool with numbers, but he was able to deal drugs out of the big safe in the back office. A brick here, brick there, turning a quick twenty grand.

He was onboard anyway to make contacts with these guys, lawyers, accountants and especially the Colombians who came into the club with a wad of cash, looking for action. Mathers was there to stroll the club as the sports hero-celeb, schmooze the girls, even turn a deal, but to watch his mouth.

So he accepted his unspoken role as a sort of glorified host-pimp. A football hero. Then again, Majors liked to hire his former pro football friends. A couple of linemen and linebackers were even now watching the floor.

Mathers was feeling pretty damn good about the setup. He was blessed, all right, the picture perfect specimen of manhood, smile, looks, talent. He had the world by the balls.

He poured another drink, did another line. Depression was for those who couldn't cut it. He then started wondering how he would approach the new girls. Well, the glass pipe was in the safe, along with ten bricks. Chicks loved rock. Get them smoked up, and he could do anything he wanted with them.

He was looking through the cameras—then he saw him.

One look and something icy grabbed his bowels. Fear, pure and simple. Why?

He peered at the video monitors and spotted the bulge beneath the guy's sports coat. The dark jacket was a little too long, a little too big. The big man had to be carrying a piece under the coat.

The guy was a problem.

In less than five seconds, Mathers had the pile of powder stashed in a locked drawer in his desk. He knew a cop when he saw one. Still, there was something in the big guy's face that told him this was no cop. He was something else, but Mathers wasn't quite sure what.

The dark-haired man was looking up, right into the cameras. Was that a slight smile Mathers saw on the man's face? The big guy moved right past his men, then past the bar, not even glancing around.

Something didn't feel right.

The big guy wasn't only a problem, Mathers decided, he was trouble. And he was headed toward the office.

Ricky Mathers was pulling a 9 mm Glock 17 pistol out of his desk when the office door exploded in a volcanic spray of wood and blood. The blood, he glimpsed, came from the crushed nose of Ritchie Stack. The former offensive tackle was flying through the air as if he weighed nothing.

Before he knew it, Mathers found himself staring

into a pair of blue eyes that didn't give a damn about his NFL career. One glance, and the football player knew this guy's heroics were real.

Still, Mathers had to try.

He swung the autopistol on target, then felt a sledgehammer hit him square in the mouth. He crashed to the floor, tasting blood.

IT WAS A ROUNDUP, hardball style.

Two steps inside the strip club, and the Executioner had made a beeline straight for the office. Instinct told him he was being closely monitored by the cameras, and he felt the eyes of maybe ten bouncers drilling into the sides of his head. Bulges of side arms were noticeable under the various coats of the security force.

Bolan ignored the suspicious looks he received from the bouncers.

The music was loud. The entire club was glittering and lit up. Glass, polished marble and gold covered everything. With the crowd fueled on booze and lust all around him, Bolan gave his surroundings a quick search. One big guard with a walkie-talkie leaned against the railing on the second floor, watching Bolan carefully, but the soldier walked on.

Bolan knew all about Ricky Mathers, former darling of the NFL. He'd been washed out of pro ball because of the very product he was now suspected of dealing out of his back office. The guy was scum.

The soldier intended to drop this gift into the DEA's lap when he was finished. Call it a peace offering, he thought, well aware the DEA wasn't going to appreciate an alleged special agent from the Justice Department, storming into Miami, kicking ass and taking names. And with carte blanche, backed by Brognola, whose clout could reach all the way to the chief executive if it had to.

A huge blond bodyguard was standing outside the office when Bolan entered the narrow hallway. The soldier wasn't about to flash his Justice Department ID to get himself inside the office. How it played out was up to Mathers and his goon squad. If there was any sizeable cache of drugs inside, Bolan would seize it. The idea was to make some more noise, make the Tartaglia Family think it was a straight rip-off of its prized strip club. After what had happened earlier in Miami Beach, Bolan knew Don Paolo would be squirming even more in confusion. Fingers might start pointing at each other or at rivals in the drug trade. Deals might even go sour from paranoia. But Bolan didn't think the narcotraffickers would close down shop. No, the savages would attempt to carry on with business as usual until they were six feet under. That was the nature of the beast.

Closing on the big goon, Bolan opened his coat a little, showing the man his Desert Eagle, but he didn't reach for it.

"Open the door, then step back."

The guard seemed unfazed. He nodded, reached for the doorknob, then made his move. Bolan saw the man's shoulders tense right before the hardman launched a roundhouse for his head. Ducking, the Executioner felt the knuckles graze the top of his skull. The hardman was quick, throwing every ounce of his solid three hundred pounds into the attack. In the next instant the goon crushed some bones in his hand when he missed and buried his fist into the wall. The soldier speared his fingers hard into the guy's stomach. A guttural belch of air exploded from the goon's mouth, and Bolan quickly followed by smashing the man's face off the wall. Blood sprayed the air from his pulped nose, but the Executioner wasn't finished.

Grabbing the guard by his shoulders, Bolan hauled him back, then used him as a battering ram. Running the guy forward, the Executioner hurled him into the door. The man's weight and Bolan's motion blasted a hole through the door, and sent the goon flying into the office.

The soldier surged through the broken doorway. The shock on the former pro baller's face was short-lived. One straight right to the man's mouth and Bolan sent him flying over his desk, Glock and paperwork taking to the air.

The bodyguard staggered to his feet, blood streaming down his face. Pivoting, the Executioner drilled a snapkick into the goon's jaw. Bone shattered and the lights went out in the giant's eyes. He collapsed at Bolan's feet.

Out in the hallway, Bolan heard the heavy pounding of footsteps. The Desert Eagle was out and aimed at the doorway. The first big shadow appeared just as the soldier snatched up Mathers. The ex-Pro Bowler was sputtering through a mouth full of blood and broken teeth, whining about his face. Bolan spun Mathers in front of him, making a human shield.

The figure in the doorway, armed with a pistol, was tracking Bolan but froze.

"Back it up," the soldier growled, jamming the muzzle of the stainless-steel hand cannon against the side of his hostage's head. "Get outside and stay there. All I want is your boy here and whatever he's got in the safe. Do it now."

The goon cursed Bolan.

"Do it, Sam!" Mathers wailed. "Jesus, don't do anything crazy. Back off, tell the others! We don't need the cops here."

"Ricky, I'm here to tell you, I never thought much of your pretty boy ass anyway. If I let this guy walk out of here, the cops will be the least of our problems. You got any idea who you're trying to rip off, asshole?"

"A scumbag by the name of Paul Tartaglia?" Bolan posed.

"You're a dead man, mister."

"Do what he wants, Sam," Mathers pleaded.

He cursed, but Bolan saw the bouncer step out of the doorway.

"Whatever's in the safe, I want it," Bolan said. "Make it quick and painless on yourself."

"Okay, okay, but Sam's right. You're either stupid or you're stone-cold crazy. You don't rip off the Tartaglias and make the next sunrise. You dumb bastard, these guys aren't even going to let you walk out of here. Half of them are Tartaglia gunmen. They're crazy. They'd just as soon shoot the whole

goddamn place up than let you leave with Don Paolo's stuff.''

''You better hope they're damn good shots then,
because you'll be the first to go, Ricky.''

Bolan hauled Mathers toward a waterbed. One
eye on the doorway, Bolan peeled the cover off a
huge pillow, then slapped it in Mathers's face.
''Let's fill this with a gift to me from the Don.''

When the ex-football player was just about to
open the safe, Bolan jerked him aside but kept him
close. One glance in the large safe and the soldier
saw at least ten bricks of cocaine and stacks of
rubber-banded hundred-dollar bills. There was also
a gun, which Bolan took and slipped into his
waistband.

While Mathers filled the pillowcase, still blubbering threats, Bolan watched the door. The loud music
was still playing, and the cameras told Bolan the
dancers and the patrons didn't have a clue what was
going on in the office. But the monitors did show
Bolan the security force was gearing up for him to
emerge. He even saw two guys talking on handheld
radios, one of them bringing a mini-Uzi into sight
but trying to keep it low.

Bolan ordered Mathers to stay in front of him at
all times. Now the tough part—getting out. In a way,
the soldier had misjudged the situation. He had no
doubt what Mathers had claimed about the security
force was true. There was a good chance the hardmen would just as soon start shooting up the place
than let him leave with the Don's coke and cash.
More than just their jobs were on the line. Given

what had happened on the beach, Bolan could be sure the Don wouldn't be in a very forgiving mood.

Nearing the splintered doorway, the Desert Eagle nuzzled against the base of Mathers's skull, Bolan shouted, "We're coming out. I want to hear gun metal hitting the floor now. Back up and give me a lot of room."

Through the pulsing rock music, the soldier heard Sam give the orders and heard metal clattering to the floor. But there was still something in the man's voice Bolan didn't trust. It was happening too easy.

The Executioner shoved Mathers through the door, then ushered him down the hall. Six grim faces were backing up, hands held in front of them.

"Don't do it like this," Mathers pleaded. "Go out the back door. You got what you wanted."

"I kind of like going public, go out the same way I came in—front door, Ricky. Relax, the goal line is in sight."

In the corner of his eye, Bolan caught the scowling faces and told them to back off. Reluctantly, they moved back, granting Bolan more room to exit the hall, onto the club floor. The soldier slapped the pillowcase against Mathers's stomach, telling him to hold it. When the ex-football player took it, Bolan locked his elbow around Mathers's throat.

Someone gasped to Bolan's side. A woman wearing nothing more than a garter stuffed with money started screaming when she saw the hand cannon against Mathers's head.

The soldier was at the edge of the bar, when the customers looked up, fear in their eyes. They started backing off. Bolan looked up, seeing one of the hardmen trying to draw a bead on him with his mini-Uzi.

The girls stopped dancing. Playtime and the hustle were over.

Bolan spun Mathers in all directions, turning when someone charged his blind side. At the last possible instant, he realized he hadn't been able to keep the bouncer in view because of the crowd of patrons skittering away from the bar.

Mathers screamed, ''No!'' a second before the bouncer bulled his massive body into Bolan.

Before he could react, the Executioner found himself airborne. He flew over the bar, crashing into glass. Then he saw the figures surging toward him, weapons drawn.

3

Beating the odds in combat, Bolan knew, was a combination of heart, skill and experience. Two of the first three, a man either pretty much had, thanks to nature, or he didn't. And experience was something learned and, more often than not, earned the hard way.

Bullying his way into the Tartaglia strip club had worked up to a point. But the soldier had miscalculated the depth of fierce loyalty of the hired help for their lord and master, Don Paolo.

Adrenaline cleared his senses as he shook his head and felt the glass slivers fall from his hair. Scuffling then sounded, loud and clear, from both ends of the bar.

Whether the hired guns were crazy enough to just start blasting away and risk mowing down patrons and dancers was something Bolan suspected he was going to wait to find out. Cutting down innocents to save his own skin wasn't Bolan's way. It never had been, and he wasn't about to start now. Without honor, without respect for innocent life and noncombatants, a man was no better than the savage or the barbarian who lived for nothing more than his own wants and needs.

Drawing the Beretta, Bolan looked up and saw he was flanked by two bartenders. One was a blond female in a skimpy outfit. Wanting nothing to do with this situation, she began to slowly back away. But the male drink-slinger was making a move as if he were going to haul Bolan up and slap him, and maybe make himself a name with the Don. Then the bartender spotted the weapon in Bolan's hand and backpedaled with nervous haste, holding his hands out as if they could ward off any bullets. So much for his tough guy routine.

"Get out of the way, Donny!" someone growled at the bartender. "Or you could be as dead as that asshole!"

They were going to gun him down, Bolan knew, as soon as they had a clear line of fire. To complicate matters even more, the soldier saw Mathers at his feet. The ex-football player had also been launched over the bar, to land in a bed of shattered bottles. Blood trickled from his blond mane as Mathers shook his head, clambering to his hands and knees. The ex-wide receiver took one look at Bolan and started skittering away before the soldier could snatch him again.

But Bolan already had the situation read and weighed in a heartbeat, and there was nothing to do now but act fast and deadly.

Then a large figure leapt onto the bar, a .357 Magnum revolver drawn and tracking Bolan. The soldier had caught enough of a glimpse of his earlier human battering ram to know that face of feral rage looming above him.

The Executioner wasted no time making his statement. He triggered the Beretta 93-R and cored a 9 mm slug through the hardman's nose. Its upward trajectory went through soft tissue before exiting out the back of the guy's skull in a burst of gray and red. The hardman followed the gory halo in a backward launch, his bulk hammering two swarthy guys in Armani suits to the floor.

Now both bartenders hit the ground, since dealing with sudden death was beyond their job descriptions. Behind the male tender, Bolan nailed two more goons, putting one 9 mm projectile each right between their eyes.

Shrill female screams erupted everywhere. Lust turned to terror, in both movement and sounds of panic. The whole floor exploded into a blind stampede of suits and naked flesh charging for the nearest exit.

Whirling, Bolan was forced to duck as glass shattered behind him. The minefield of exploding liquor bottles and mirrors, he saw, was due from the mini-Uzi chattering in the hands of the hardman near the railing on the second level.

"Get out of the goddamn way, Mathers, you little punk!"

A glance to his left flank, and Bolan found a hardforce of three goons, bumping and shoving their way through the crowd. The human stampede would buy Bolan a few critical seconds. The soldier crouched beneath the counter as glass and liquid kept erupting over his head.

The soldier turned his deathsights on three gunmen at the other end of the bar. Mathers stood between Bolan and the hardmen, frozen in fear. The ex-wide receiver shrieked when he turned and saw Bolan's Beretta spitting flame and lead past his face. Crouched and shooting around Mathers, the Executioner marched a line of slugs across the chests of the trio in lightning succession. One by one they spun, their aimless bullets pumping into the mirrors behind the bar.

Before Mathers could flee, Bolan clipped the man over the head with his Beretta. The blow unintentionally saved the ex-football player's life. As Mathers collapsed in front of Bolan, bottles exploded right where he'd just stood.

Dropping to the floor, below the tracking line of fire, Bolan made his way toward the opposite end of the bar. Customers were still screaming and flailing for escape. The soldier came up and drilled a goon near the stairs in the chest. Above the guard, a couple of suits were rolling, head over heels, down the steps. Everywhere the crush of bodies was a moving wall of innocents, a barrier that forced Bolan's fire in check for the moment.

The Executioner ducked a millisecond before a volley from the mini-Uzi sizzled over his head, slugs skidding off the bartop, shattering more glass. He moved ahead, gauging the distance and position of the gunner leaning against the railing. Popping up, Bolan watched as money, bottles and ashtrays went flying through the air, and tables upended as bouncers with guns took out anything that stood in their way.

The Executioner spotted the gunner with the mini-Uzi slap a fresh clip home. It was now or never.

Slugs whizzed past Bolan's head from the gunmen attempting a flanking maneuver across the floor. Their autopistols fired, but two unsuspecting patrons absorbed the bullets for Bolan, their skulls blasted open in front of the Executioner's face. The guard team yelled curses as the bodies halted their killing intent.

Bolan aimed and triggered his Beretta as the gunner upstairs cocked the bolt on his mini-Uzi. Three 9 mm Parabellum slugs drilled through the hardman's upper chest. The gunman started twisting as he fell, his finger locked on the trigger. The wild spray of lead from the dying man's weapon hit the ceiling, and an avalanche of glass shards rained on the stampeding crowd. One giant sheet broke over the head of a guard who was lining Bolan up with his Heckler & Koch MP-5 submachine gun. The man crashed to the marble floor, blood seeping from his twitching body. He looked like a pin cushion of glass needles.

Bolan leathered the Beretta and hauled out the mammoth .44 Magnum Desert Eagle. Tracking on, the Executioner held his ground, triggering deadly precision rounds that swept two more gun-toting hardmen off their feet. For the next few moments, the raging sea of fleeing bodies kept Bolan from chancing anymore Desert Eagle fire. Likewise, the few remaining hardmen were too busy dodging bodies and trying to bull their way toward Bolan to be able to line him up with accurate weapons fire.

Hunched and on the move, Bolan found he had somehow held on to the Don's stash when he'd been launched over the bar. He scooped up the pillowcase and jacked a blubbering Mathers to his feet. A shard of mirror exploded just behind Bolan. A quick sweep of the dance floor and the soldier found a dark-haired giant with a .44 Magnum revolver thundering away. One squeeze of the Desert Eagle's trigger and Bolan nearly decapitated the hardman, sending him flying through a trio of silk suits with aloha shirts. Two more roars from the Desert Eagle and Bolan sent one gunner through a glass partition.

The soldier slapped the pillowcase against Mathers's chest. "Hold this and don't run from me or I'll shoot you."

Grabbing Mathers by the shoulder, the Executioner hauled the man away from the bar.

Checking the rear, Bolan found nothing but utter pandemonium. With the stampede behind him, it would guide him to the exit, hidden by the mass of people.

Outside, Bolan kept moving with the racing crowd through the parking lot. A few blocks north, near the Dolphin Expressway, his rented Ford Taurus was parked in a vacant lot.

"Now what?" Mathers asked.

"Just keep moving and don't do anything stupid," Bolan warned.

Chaos was thinning behind the soldier as he led

his prisoner along. Tire rubber screeched in the palm tree-lined lot that fanned out in front of Tartaglia's exclusive strip club. No gunmen were trailing him. Sometimes, Bolan thought, the bull wins.

THE EXECUTIONER HAD a decision to make about Ricky Mathers.

Ten minutes behind the wheel, driving slowly south by southwest through Miami, Bolan found himself in the Latino part of town. With nightfall approaching and stifling heat over the city, Bolan purposely headed deeper into a part of town where no gringo should be after dark.

Mathers was clearly uncomfortable with his surroundings. Seated beside Bolan, his hands cuffed in front of him, the ex-football player looked at all the iron-barred storefronts and the people scuffling along the sidewalks as if he wanted to disappear. Bolan had plans for Mathers but his decision wasn't that cut and dry.

Bolan drove the Ford Taurus south on Teddy Roosevelt Avenue. Latino music and reggae throbbed in the night, adding tension to the silence between the soldier and the former football hero. In that part of town, Bolan was pretty sure they'd be left alone. He had dark hair, but he could never pass for Latino. He was too big, too white and his eyes were too icy blue. No, the traffickers and the predators of these streets would steer clear of him simply because he looked like a big gringo cop. For the time being that was good enough. As for the blond

Mathers, well, he might look like a piece of prime rib to the Spanish street toughs.

Bolan gave the former NFL star a sideways glance. He felt utter contempt for Mathers. The guy had sold his soul long ago and indulged his dark side by taking the easy way and turning his back on a life of promise and potential. Bolan saw through the guy as easily as he could look through a pane of glass. Once a star in the public arena of fame and easy money, Mathers had existed in a world where guys were overpaid and overglorified. Indeed, the Blond Jet came from a place that was as remote from the world of Mack Bolan as heaven was to hell. Just a sign of the times, the soldier decided.

Mathers fidgeted as shadows called out from the sidewalks in Spanish. No doubt, the nightlife around Bolan was hustling some of Don Paolo's product, eager for money to ease the misery of poverty and desperation. The shadows selling crack would never get the first inch of slack from Bolan. Men had choices, and they made the wrong one.

"You have any idea where you are, fella?" Mathers croaked.

"Not really." Bolan cocked a wry grin. "I'm just a tourist, passing through."

The problem the soldier faced was to either dump Mathers off in the lap of his DEA contact, or to cut him loose. Taking the coke bricks and cash was a message, not a rip-off, but it wouldn't hurt to play the angle of a loose cannon in town looking to take what the Don held so near and dear. Not only that, but Bolan figured Mathers would run straight back to the club, or call Don Paolo himself to report the damage. The ex-football player had served his purpose. Maybe the Don would think Mathers was part of some elaborate setup gone bad. Maybe the Blond Jet would suffer a fate worse than death at the hands of the Don who had been humiliated twice in one day.

Mathers tried to put some bluster into his voice. "Okay, tough guy. Well, my suggestion would be for you to clear out of Miami, maybe even vanish from the country. You don't steal from Paul Tartaglia and live to finish the week."

Bolan would have to lose the rental car. Mathers was scared, and not too bright even, but he wasn't that stupid. The former NFL darling would give his boss the make and license number of the Ford Taurus.

The Executioner drove into an alley and parked. "I'm not going anywhere." Quickly, Bolan uncuffed Mathers. "But you're free to go. Slick-looking guy like you shouldn't have any trouble getting a cab down here."

"Yeah, if I can even find one."

"So walk. But when you see your boss, the big boss, not Majors, I want you to relay a message to him. Listen closely. Don Paolo has twenty-four hours to dismantle his cocaine empire and turn himself over to the DEA or the Grim Reaper will visit him in the dead of night. White Christmas in Miami is over." Bolan made Mathers repeat the message back to him, word for word. The ex-NFL star stumbled over a couple of words until Bolan pointed the business end of the Desert Eagle at him. "One more time. Get it right."

Mathers got it straight verbatim the second time. "Are you a cop?"

The soldier gave the ex-NFL hero a cold smile. "I just told you who I was. Now, get out."

The guy hopped out and Bolan drove off down the alley. He looked in his rearview mirror, saw the shadow of the Blond Jet hero fade. Something told Bolan it was the last time he would ever see Ricky Mathers.

He then decided to readjust his game plan before meeting his DEA contact. One more stop, this time, north up I-95. In roughly twenty minutes, the Executioner would round up a potential star songbird for the DEA. After the havoc he had wreaked, the soldier figured it was the least he could do for the home team fighting the war on drugs.

AT FIRST GLANCE, the new condos, motels and hotels lining the beachfronts between Hollywood and Fort Lauderdale appeared as if they were trying to upscale and upgrade the image of the two towns from one wild party to swank but peaceful for tourists. Lush tropical vegetation sprung up around fancy cafés and restaurants, everything looking pink or blue and finely scrubbed. But all the money men in South Florida couldn't change the reality of Fort Lauderdale, Bolan realized, as he headed west on Sunrise Boulevard after swinging off I-95.

In short order, the strip joints and seedy bars began to appear. There were more than a few shadows lurking the streets. Painted women in tight shorts or black leather miniskirts hugged the various corners.

Bolan drove on, shaking his head. They could call the crimes of prostitution and drug-use victimless crimes all they wanted, but he knew better.

No one, not even Mack Bolan, could completely and single-handedly wipe out the narcotics menace that was now entrenched in the land as part of the American culture. But he could try to do his part. Even if his efforts saved a few lives...well, the risk to gain even a little edge over the dealers of misery and death was worth it.

The address of the white stucco, one-story house in a tight residential area in West Lauderdale had been given to Bolan by Hal Brognola. The DEA had a lead on one Artie Fromer, but the man just seemed to have disappeared when they were closing on his operation after a couple of key busts. Then, two days ago, Fromer had called the agency from a pay phone. He wanted to come in as part of the Witness Protection Program. The would-be snitch gave a temporary address to the DEA man, who had passed it to Brognola as part of the mutual cooperation within the Justice Department. Two days could be an eternity in the life of a guy like Fromer.

Bolan hoped he wasn't too late.

Especially when he saw the house was dark, the front door open and a four-door sedan was parked out front.

The Executioner slid his Ford Taurus beside some brush at the end of the street and killed the lights and engine. He stepped out of the car, his senses assaulted by heat and the ceaseless buzz of insects and the croak of frogs. Drawing the Beretta, a fresh clip in place, he threaded the sound suppressor onto the muzzle. He closed on the house, instinctively knowing something was wrong.

It was a quiet neighborhood, and at that time of night there wasn't a soul around. Air conditioners were on in each home, suburbanites settling in for the evening. Everybody should be minding their own business. He hoped.

So far the soldier's campaign hadn't been interrupted by the police.

Bearing down on the snitch's house, Bolan knew that could soon change. Crouched and stalking low along the lush vegetation in front of the house, Bolan heard angry voices coming through the doorway.

"You're lying to us, bitch. You got enough coke here to light up half the city. Where's Artie hiding? You got some secret hole in the closet where the little maggot's tucked away?"

"I told you, he left hours ago."

The sound of flesh striking flesh echoed through the doorway.

"Look, Artie says he'll return the stuff if you just let him—"

"Shut your mouth. Benny, go close the damn door. What the hell's the matter with you anyway? We got some work to do here on this little slut."

Bolan inched closer to the door. It was most definitely a bonus that he had arrived when he had. He needed Fromer alive. The man had all the key knowledge about the Tartaglia operation. And whomever the woman was, Bolan wasn't about to let the hardmen have their way with her.

There was only one way to do it. Through the soft glow of light he saw the shape coming toward the doorway.

Bolan sighted the Beretta as the shadow stepped into view.

4

Bolan thought about trying to take the man alive. The soldier had too many questions burning for answers. Who exactly were the invaders? How had they found Fromer's hideout? How many were in the house, or perhaps in the neighborhood, waiting to roll up once they received word their boy was bagged?

He never got the chance. The big guy in the black sports shirt and white slacks was alert to the soldier's sudden presence. A stainless-steel revolver began to swing Bolan's way when the Executioner stroked the Beretta's trigger. No sooner was one 9 mm hollowpoint bullet released from the sound-suppressed muzzle than a neat hole appeared between the Mob man's eyes, and Bolan was surging through the door.

Bolan found himself in a shabby and sparsely furnished living room where the big attraction for the home's occupant was most likely the pile of powder cocaine on a mirror on the coffee table.

Soft lamplight cast ghostly hues over the savage intent on the face of a stocky dark-haired man brandishing a .357 Magnum revolver. The man reacted quickly to Bolan's violent intrusion.

The Executioner was sweeping past the crumpled form in the doorway, drawing target acquisition, when the hardman reeled in the skinny brunette. The soldier nosedived to the floor, just in case the guy decided to start blasting. The Executioner slid up behind the couch, came up with the Beretta in a two-fisted grip and aimed at the man's scowling features.

"Lose the gun, pal! Or the coke slut gets her head blown off!" the man rasped, sticking the muzzle of the revolver in the woman's ear. Tough pro that he was, the hardman kept the woman as a perfect human shield between himself and Bolan.

The woman cried, "Please, mister, do as he says! These guys are Mafia, they're crazy!"

"Shut your mouth, you lousy coke whore!" the button man snarled, hauling the woman back a step.

At least Bolan had confirmation of the enemy. But how had the Mafia found Fromer so easily? Had the would-be snitch gotten careless and been spotted somewhere in Miami? Then there was another, even more nightmarish scenario. And that was the probability Tartaglia had someone in the DEA on his payroll.

Answers had to wait. Right now, the Executioner couldn't afford to waste time in a standoff. He was aiming the Beretta as the guy shouted at him to drop the gun, when a shadow barreled out of the hall closet.

Bolan had never laid eyes on Artie Fromer, but

he supposed the Mafia killers had been right when they'd believed the snitch was hiding in a closet.

The Mafia gunner spotted the threat charging his blind side, and Bolan was set to pump one 9 mm slug through his brain. But the woman was either so jacked up on coke or so terrified of death, that she got into the foray.

The goon pulled his .357 pistol away from the woman's head only an instant before she slashed her elbow into his mouth. Wheeling, not missing a heartbeat, she started pummeling his face with clenched fists. Then the figure Bolan assumed was Fromer bulldozed into the hit man. There was such tremendous impact from the snitch's charge that all three tumbled to the floor in a tangled heap of flailing arms and legs.

For a split second, the hit man slung Fromer off, leaving Bolan a clean line of fire. Without hesitation, the Executioner seized the opportunity and cored one 9 mm projectile through the button man's skull.

Now Bolan only had to deal with the two fear-crazed and coke-wired threats. The woman came at the soldier like a wildcat. He saw the roundhouse punch telegraphed right before she launched it. He ducked, feeling the air swish overhead. Reacting, feeling none too chivalrous and glimpsing Fromer going for the revolver, Bolan cracked an uppercut off the brunette's jaw. He put just enough force into the blow to drop her on her back, groggy and dazed but breaking no bones. Just as Fromer's fingers touched the pistol, the soldier drilled a 9 mm hole into the floor at the feet of the snitch.

"Don't do it, Artie," Bolan growled. "I'm not the Mob."

Fromer thought about it, then reached out for the .357 Magnum revolver.

Bolan drilled another slug into the floor. "Don't be stupid, Artie. If I'd wanted you dead, you would be already. I can get a little ugly, if you want."

Fromer shook with fear and racing adrenaline. Up close, Bolan saw the snitch wasn't much to look at, slightly built, with soft features and neatly trimmed brown hair. His blue eyes were bloodshot and dilated from long hours of snorting coke. Hopped up on coke or not, Fromer had shown courage, and Bolan made a mental note to keep his guard up around him.

"Who the hell are you, then?"

The Executioner loomed over Fromer, scooped up the revolver and tucked it in his waistband. "Your savior."

Bolan showed him his Justice Department credentials, but Fromer didn't look impressed.

"Right. How do I know that's real? How do I know you won't just drag me down to the river and shoot me?"

"Right now, you don't have a choice but to trust me. Get the woman. You'll drive, she'll ride with you in front. Let's move."

"Okay, big guy. Relax, I'm with you," Fromer relented, then looked at the pile of cocaine, a flicker of hope in his eyes.

As if to answer Fromer's unspoken question, the

Executioner pumped three rounds into the mirror, spewing white powder all over the living room.

The snitch looked set to erupt with rage, but Bolan held his ground, his face as hard as steel. Fromer seemed to shrink before the soldier with renewed fear.

"The party's over, Artie."

"FIRST OFF, let me tell you something, Belasko. When I pledged full one-hundred-percent cooperation with the Justice Department, that didn't mean I'd let Washington come down here and start a full-scale war on the streets of Miami."

Bolan watched as his contact, Special Agent Richard Tasker, in charge of the DEA Organized Crime Task Force, paced around the large table. Tasker was a broad-shouldered, six-footer with closely cropped black hair and dark brooding eyes.

For reasons somewhat strange and unknown to Bolan, the task force had taken two suites of the four-star Hotel Inter-Continental Miami as its temporary command center. From their thirty-fourth floor penthouse, Bolan had a clear view across the bay to the towering condos and hotels of Miami Beach. Palm trees and wicker chairs were spread around the large room. The floors were white marble, everything colored in soft gray or beige. Posh accommodations, all right, certainly not standard operating procedure for the DEA.

Bolan figured since times had changed in the war on drugs, the DEA had to change too. With all the seizures of drugs, cash and property in recent years, it stood to reason that Uncle Sam was looking to upscale operations, both on the battlefield and behind the scenes. Maybe the idea was to keep pace with the traffickers, in money and style, by allowing agents to look more like their glitzy counterparts. Window dressing might give agents more of a fighting chance to blend into the fast, high-flying lifestyle of their adversaries, but it was a double-edged sword, of course. If the borderline agent got the taste of the poison the drug world offered, he could be more than tempted to abandon ship and go for himself. Given what had happened at Fromer's hideout, Bolan suspected the worst of the home team. It was unfortunate that a man would go to the other side out of pure greed, but it happened.

The Executioner sat at the table, with Jack Grimaldi beside him. Stony Man's ace pilot looked a little chastised. Bolan, known now to the entire task force as Special Agent Mike Belasko, had already gotten up-to-speed on "Agent Griswald's" situation. Special Agent Brockton had taken the honors, recapping how Grimaldi had blown a major bust of a Tartaglia warehouse that had been under DEA surveillance for weeks. Following his boom of displeasure at both Bolan and Grimaldi, Brockton had elected to pace the living room. He was now chomping on a cigar while four other agents pored over files and intel. Wall maps of Miami, Miami Beach, and one showing all of South Florida were hung from the wall in the far corner of the living room. One agent was circling areas on the map with a red marker. Another was hunched over an all-glass coffee table, stacking the coke bricks and counting the wads of cash Bolan had seized from Baby Doll Heaven. There were a lot of sport shirts and aloha shirts in the suite, along with some silk slacks, alligator belts and shoes. But every agent wore a shoulder-holstered Glock pistol, with a couple of assault rifles leaning in corners of the room.

It had been a short but anxious drive back to Miami for Bolan. Both Fromer and his girlfriend, Candy, had fidgeted and complained the entire trip while Bolan sat in the back, poised for trouble to break loose from either inside the Taurus or from Tartaglia's goons who might be on the lookout for his vehicle. There had been no time to ditch the wheels and rent another vehicle. But Bolan figured Mathers hadn't had enough time to report back to Don Paolo yet. Fromer and his girl were now locked away in the adjoining bedroom, awaiting their verdict.

At that moment Bolan had no choice but to take a little heat, to allow Special Agents Tasker and Brockton to let off some righteous steam.

From the DEA's point of view, their anger made sense to Bolan. Of course, the drug enforcers had no idea that he and Grimaldi had rolled into town to aid the war on drugs in their own blazing way—which was take no prisoners, show no mercy.

But the DEA had to be brought into the game plan in some official manner. The last thing Bolan or Grimaldi needed was to be tripping over agency operations, risk friendly fire, or accidentally cut down an agent. Either way, Bolan would only tell Tasker about their mission on a need-to-know basis. At this point, the soldier sensed the situation with the DEA could turn ugly. Especially since he had filled Tasker in on his trouble at Baby Doll Heaven, and what had gone down with the roundup of Fromer. The only part of his day he left out was his opening round of war against Tartaglia on Miami Beach. Sniping off the Don's button men and two main drug distributors would definitely be pushing his luck with the DEA.

"Ten keys, and a little over a hundred grand in cash," Brockton announced from the living room. "It's a grain of sand on the beach, but Tartaglia will be more pissed by the way it was taken, by some cowboy, than miss a few kilos." Brockton scowled around his cigar. "Don't mind me if I skip patting you on the back. See, the problem I've got with this, Belasko, is obvious. First of all, this afternoon Tartaglia was hit by a sniper while he did his beach thing. Word is five guys, including two main distributors of Miami's godfather, bought it, burned down with one shot apiece. It sounds like a real pro carried it off to me, but I guess you wouldn't know anything about that, would you?"

When Bolan said nothing, Brockton grunted, then continued, "A little while later, Agent Griswald uses a frigging bazooka to blow a half dozen guys into so many pieces, it might take us days to identify them. About the same time Agent Griswald is declaring Armageddon, you bulldoze your way into the Don's strip club and shoot the place all to hell, endangering innocent lives. I don't give a shit if the place was crawling with human cockroaches. Not everyone was dealing dope. I guess you're going to sit there and tell me you didn't shoot until someone shot at you first, huh?''

Bolan met the black agent's penetrating stare and said in a level voice, "Not exactly."

"Well, then, what, 'exactly'?" Brockton growled.

"Let's just say I didn't shoot anyone unless they intended to shoot me first."

Brockton's gaze narrowed with angry disbelief. "Intended? How do you establish this intent? Are they teaching shoot to kill if the bad guys got intent these days at Quantico?"

"Let's call it hard experience. Just leave it that I shot all the right people."

Brockton was set to pursue it, but Tasker jumped in. "All right, all right, let's cut the muscle flexing here. We've got serious problems we need to get solved right now." Tasker took a cigarette and fired it up. "The problem I've got, Belasko, Griswald, is that I've been one step away from bringing down Paul Tartaglia, who is the biggest cocaine importer in South Florida. Every time we get set to nail him, he slips away. Mainly because he's put a legitimate face on himself. He knows the game well enough to dodge the big bullet coming his way.

"Now, despite what happened at the river, Griswald, I don't think it would've made much difference in us getting any closer to nailing this bastard. You see, once again, the Don plays all his cards just right. The warehouse was originally his property, but he leases it to other so-called citrus distributors.

All it means is Tartaglia's lawyers would have had a field day making assholes of the DEA. They'd say it wasn't even his warehouse at the time, how stupid are you guys in the DEA, don't you know the law? All that slick lawyer bullshit that keeps a scumbag drug dealer like Tartaglia on the streets, and has for twenty years in this town."

Tasker kept pacing, and smoked harder on his cigarette. "You know what eats my guts out? Everyone in this town knows exactly who and what Tartaglia is. I mean, this guy even insists his people address him as Don Paolo, even the reporters on the evening news, as if it's a big joke, a game. He throws a bunch of drug money into charities and hospitals, builds condos, hotels and everyone treats the guy like he's some kind of modern-day Robin Hood. Go figure."

"We live in some real fucked up times," Brockton snarled, "I grew up, gentlemen, in this city, in Overtown. I've seen firsthand what drugs do to whole families. How specific do I need to get? You want to hear about mothers whoring themselves for a ten-dollar rock or selling their own sons and daughters so they can pay off their drug debt? You want to hear about twelve-year-old kids who just as soon kill a cop than get busted? This crap has ruined entire communities. The problem is, you don't hear about what's happening with this war on the news anymore because drugs have become so deeply rooted in our society, it's not newsworthy. Hell, buying this garbage has become as easy as walking to a convenience store and buying a six-pack."

Brockton stubbed out his cigar before continuing. "If something isn't done about it, in five years we'll be seeing an entire generation of sociopaths out on the streets, living for drugs, drug money and ready to kill or be killed by the barrel of a gun."

Bolan knew the reality all too well. That was why he was long overdue for a trip to Miami.

Hard silence followed Brockton's words.

Tasker seemed to think about something, then said, "Okay, here we are. In some ways we're ahead on points. Tartaglia's going to be nervous. He might figure he's getting hit from inside his organization or maybe the Cali people are looking to remove him from the picture. I really can't say either way, but he's going to have to deal with the cops. Standard questions, well, you know the drill. I seriously doubt, however, Tartaglia will crawl into a hole and just ride this out. Fact is, you two might have helped dig out all the scumbags and get them into high gear where we can nail them once and for all."

"In other words, thanks for the help, gentlemen," Brockton gruffed. "A shooting war in the streets of Miami may do the job for us."

Bolan ignored the agent's anger. "He has a brother, Sal, right?" the soldier asked Tasker. "What's his story?"

"His younger brother, Sal," Tasker answered, "is pretty much a nonfactor anymore. The man's lived high and hard for years. Word is, he likes his own product, the booze and his call girls. Right now, he's living, or slowly dying, if you will, in his Palm Beach estate, from some, uh, mysterious illness. It's all being kept real secretive, but I'd bet he didn't use his little raincoat when he spent a night in heaven with a thousand-dollar hooker.

"The Tartaglia brothers were once the force to be reckoned with in this town, but that was before the Medellín then the Cali scumbags showed up. The big buzz from our own informants is that two brothers from Cali, the Rodrigo brothers, Juan Carlos and Fernando, have been meeting with Tartaglia. Whether it was their dope we've seized offshore the past few weeks, I couldn't tell you. But right now we're seeing a whole lot of heroin out there.

"Word is, the Rodrigo brothers are not only the new players in town, but they have a chop-and-step factory somewhere, chemists who are looking to produce a smokeable rock form of heroin, or a mix of cocaine and heroin to be smoked, commonly known as a speedball. I don't need to tell you the fallout of that if they're successful. So far, we've come up cold on any leads to this factory. The Rodrigos have several legitimate businesses, which goes without saying, are fronts. They've got a restaurant in the Latin Quarter and an import business that supposedly brings in coffee. They also have a string of flower shops, of all goddamn things."

Bolan recalled Brognola mentioning a connection between Tartaglia and the Rodrigos. According to Brognola's intel, the brothers had grown up in the streets of Cali. Once petty thieves and drug runners, they later became assassins for the Cali Cartel. So far, they had never been brought to justice. Bolan needed to hear more about the Rodrigo brothers, and Tasker had to have been reading his mind.

"Yeah, they're the newest and the most dangerous import yet from Colombia. They're pretty much loose cannons, on the periphery of the Cali Cartel's operations. But someone down there either owes them favors, by way of their lives, or they've gotten the kind of twisted respect from their own. The scuttlebutt is they're in the process of importing enough heroin into South Florida to make every junkie forget crack ever existed. Fromer, the scumbag you brought in, Belasko, was close to Tartaglia's distribution network. I'm hoping he can give us some answers. Fromer will want the world if he talks to us, but at this point, I'm prepared to give him what he wants. Thing is, Belasko and Griswald, you both know how it goes. All the surveillance and phone taps in the world rarely nail these guys, at least the big sharks. You need a songbird. It's how all the major busts go down. Someone talks."

"Why don't we take it slow with him?" Bolan suggested. "Right now, he's so jacked up on coke I'm not sure I'd trust the first word that comes out of his mouth."

"We've got a twelve-pack in the refrigerator," Tasker said, grinding out his cigarette. "A few beers will take the edge off."

Bolan turned grim and chose his next words carefully. "Someone in the Tartaglia Family knew where to find him."

The insinuation flared resentment in Tasker's eyes. "What are you saying, Belasko?"

"I'm just saying we need to be careful, that's all. I'm not pointing fingers. Let's just move with some caution."

After a long silence, Tasker asked Bolan, "Okay, Belasko, since I'm ordered by my superiors to go the extra mile with you two, what exactly do you want from me?"

"Time and space. Some hard intel to move on."

Brockton cursed. "You want us to back off our operations so you two can go out there to shoot and blow up half our city?"

Grimaldi spoke for the first time. "I don't think we can promise any peaceful solution, Agent Brockton. You know the score here. To beat these people you've got to play hardball."

"Maybe I can use some persuasion," Bolan interjected, "to get them to turn themselves over in one piece."

Tasker scoffed, but the soldier already knew his bluff would be called. "Fat chance."

Bolan cut a wry grin. "Yeah. Slim to none, I'd say."

"You two have forty-eight hours," Tasker said. "I don't know what kind of clout your boss carries at the Justice Department, but my gut tells me it's considerable. Okay, let's bring our pigeon out. We'll put the facts of life to him. Belasko, you want to be the good cop or the bad cop?"

Bolan shrugged. "You want to flip a coin?"

Tasker frowned but reached inside his pocket. He

flipped the coin in the air, said, "Heads, I'm the good cop."

It landed on the table, tails. Somehow, that suited Bolan just fine.

5

Ben "Judas" Stiles was so pumped on adrenaline he believed he could almost smell all that cocaine in the steamy backcountry air of the Everglades. Tonight, he was leading the charge on what could be the biggest score of his life. If this hit was successful, it was just the balls-out kind of move that could put the Devil's Horsemen on the map, making them a monster power to be reckoned with in the drug underworld.

Eyelids closed to mere slits, the wind in his face and bug juice spattered in his beard from the short run down the Tamiami Trail from their secluded compound, Stiles swung his black 1200 cc custom-made Harley-Davidson motorcycle onto the back road. It was a cloudless night, the sky bright with countless stars and a half-moon. Anytime, he expected to see the sleek black shape of the stripped-down Learjet banking over the swampland from the south. Its lights would be off, naturally, the jet flying so low it would almost seem to scrape the tips of pine trees. Only when the jet was coming in for a landing, guided down by a couple of guys on the ground with a radio, would it then turn its lights on.

It was risky, all right, but Stiles had to admire any flyboy smugglers who could bring in such a major load, putting it all on the line for a nice little cut of the action. There was grim evidence all over the backcountry of planes that had either run out of fuel on a run or clipped the trees to crash and burn. Parts of the Everglades even looked like mass graveyards with the crushed remains or strewed wreckage of some unfortunate smuggler's aircraft.

Stiles had known more than a few drug pilots over the years. All smugglers flew by the seat of their pants, usually fast and low over the ocean, almost skimming the surface, sometimes even flying in the worst of weather, knowing the Coast Guard wouldn't risk the lives of their own, or jeopardize an expensive government ship for just one plane. There were always more planes, Stiles thought, grinning against the wind. Then again, he knew the cocaine barons from South America had more money than most Third World countries, and the latest state-of-the-art technology was but throwing away mere pennies. That kind of money meant power to Stiles, and that meant control. It was just one reason why he wanted a piece of that kind of fantastic action.

After all, cocaine was still the craved drug of choice out there. In fact, the word from a number of his own sources in the trade was that cocaine was as big as ever. Hell, the price of a kilo was around ten grand these days, a gram of powder a mere seventy bucks, all dirt cheap prices for any addict serious about his or her using. It meant there was more than enough powder and rock candidates on the streets to go around for an industrious, ambitious guy like himself.

Not to mention heroin was becoming the latest rage on the streets, making a strong comeback. He wanted to be a part of it.

Making crystal methane at the club's compound was too risky. Why chance making dope then running it to Atlanta or New Orleans himself when he could easily pick up the finished product? Crank whacked out too many people anyway, far worse than crack or powder cocaine. One bust of a user or a dealer on the lower rung of the pecking order and the cops would close in. That was how almost all dealers, large or small, went down. Someone got popped, then snitched to save himself from doing time. And Stiles was a three-time loser. Only two years out of the pen this time around, and he had already determined he'd die before going back to prison again.

The only plus he'd gained from a combined twelve years in the joint was that most of his biker club was made up of ex-cons. They either came from the Aryan Brotherhood, the Klan or the Aryan Nations. And all of them had saved one another's lives in the joint from the blacks and the Hispanics at some time. Racial pride, Stiles thought, was in short commodity these days. They were the last of a dying breed. He knew beyond any doubt all of them would go the extra mile for one another. Even if it meant death.

Feeling the powerful throb of his custom iron

horse beneath him, Stiles peeled off onto the dark, narrow dirt trail that cut a tortuous path through the cypress and mangroves of the swampland. Behind the leader of the South Florida chapter of the outlaw biker club, a force of twenty-two long-haired, bearded and wild-eyed riders in black leather and denim rumbled slowly in line on their motorcycles. The thunder of those powerful engines bolstered Stiles's confidence. Each outlaw had a swastika carved on his chest, right over his heart, done by a hunting knife. The "blood-knifing," as Stiles called it, was a ritual that was part of the initiation rights to be a member of the Devil's Horsemen. If a guy even flinched during the ritual, he'd be pummeled to a bloody pulp by the others. Once the man's flesh was cut, though, the knife that marked him became his personal fighting blade, which he would carry with him until the day he died. Tattoos and their colors meant everything of true value to all of them. And the club's emblem on the back of their jackets—a skeleton with a shotgun in hand, bursting out of a fireball on its Harley—was Stiles's own creative touch to give the club its own identity.

Proud of his men, Stiles threw a quick look over his shoulder, checking to make sure everything was still running smooth. Three black Chevy vans trailed the bikes, their lights doused while Stiles led them a quarter mile to a tight clearing near the edge of some woods. In those vans, he knew, was enough stolen government-issue hardware to field at least four determined squads of warriors with a mission. And theirs was a righteous mission, one that would net them several million dollars in cash, nail down their future, once and for all, in big-time drug moving. Of course, there'd be problems to solve the next day, but he was a leader with a solid plan. Whatever was going to happen with the Cali people who were hooked up with the Mob in Miami, well, he'd deal himself in, or he would deal them out.

First order of business was to seize the load.

Lights and engines on the bikes were killed. Stiles unfolded his lean, six-foot frame from his Harley. He smoothed back his shoulder-length black hair as men emerged from the vans. The side doors were slid open, and M-16s were handed out, along with two LAW rocket launchers. Stiles sought out the short, bearded, heavyset Colombian in the darkness.

The biker walked up to Carlos Miniguez. There was fear in the Colombian dealer's eyes, but Stiles understood the guy's predicament. The man was rolling his own people, after all. But that's how it went, Stiles knew, in the drug trade. Someone became unhappy with their lord and masters, wanted a bigger percentage or simply wanted to carve out their own turf. In this case, Miniguez was just plain scared of what was about to go down, both here and back in Miami.

For long moments, with the buzz of mosquito swarms in his ears, Stiles looked at Miniguez. The outlaw biker leader put his hands on his hips, felt the weight of the 9 mm Browning Hi-Power tucked in his waistband. Then his sergeant-in-arms, Tommy "Wildman" Thomas, handed him an M-16 and two spare clips.

"You better be damn sure about this, amigo," Stiles growled.

"How many times do I need to tell you?" Miniguez said. "I'm positive. The source inside the Rodrigo organization is reliable. The man is as unhappy about the possibility of war between rival groups as I am. I know the man personally from Cali. We both agree on one thing. If some blood must be shed tonight to keep a war from erupting in Miami, then that is the way it must be."

"So you've said. And here I thought all you Cali boys were one big happy family."

Grim chuckles sounded around Stiles. Miniguez fidgeted and looked anxious to get on with his part in the treacherous setup.

And the man had better be right about the information, Stiles thought, right down to the time of the aircraft's arrival, the numbers they'd be facing on the hit and the size of the load. Or he'd leave Miniguez floating in the swamp, so riddled with bullets there wouldn't be enough left of the guy to feed to the alligators.

But Stiles had no choice but to trust Miniguez.

The Colombian was part of a rival Cali group in Miami that was unhappy that two new Cali players, the Rodrigo brothers, had rolled into town within the past eighteen months, set up their own distribution network outside the normal cartel chain of command. It seemed the Rodrigo brothers were getting bigger every day, outplaying, outmaneuvering, hell, outlasting their competition. As a rule, the Cali people, Stiles knew from his own sources in Miami, stuck together. But the Rodrigos were obvious loose cannons who wanted their own organization, their own way, their own money. Rumor was that the Rodrigos were working out a major deal with the Tartaglia Family. Or so Miniguez said. It would be easy enough for Stiles to check out. Right now, the Cali snitch was his boy, bought and paid for.

Miniguez had key information about one method of smuggling the Rodrigos used—a simple drop on a remote field at the edge of Everglades country. The cargo was then off-loaded into waiting vans. Only this night, a hardforce of shooters from the group Miniguez moved dope for was going to be on hand to steal the Rodrigo load.

Stiles had been working on an angle to infiltrate the group Miniguez worked with for the past two months. Since the Cali snitch had a love for pretty, blond American girls, Stiles had dressed up one of the old ladies at the compound and had her frequent one of the clubs in Miami where Miniguez searched for fun. Well, he'd tasted Stiles's female poison, all right. Sex and booze had a way of loosening up the man's tongue. It seemed Miniguez was scared of losing all he had worked so hard to attain, that he was willing to jump ship to the Rodrigos. The other night, the old lady, Babs, had simply left the back door open at the man's Coral Gables home. Stiles had walked in with a couple of his men and made Miniguez an offer of help—at point-blank range. It was just the kind of break Stiles had been looking for. Now Miniguez had provided the way in for the

Devil's Horsemen to reap some of the action the biker leader so hungered to taste.

"You were very clever, *hombre*, getting the woman next to me like you did," the dealer said, an edge of resentment in his voice.

"Your mistake. A man should be more careful about showing any particular weakness. What's more, you should be more careful and watch your mouth, Carlos." Stiles cocked the bolt on the M-16, chambering the first round. "You should know better than trust a woman with your business. Hey, what's to worry anyway? You're unhappy in your situation with your people, sounds like you're long overdue for some change. Think about it for a second. Your guys are here to take the brothers' load. It's a cowboy play that'll send every gun the Rodrigos have got into the Miami streets. We're going to save the Rodrigos' dope, take it back to them with a big smile on our faces. Naturally, the brothers will know there's a snake slithering around in their organization. Some heads will roll, but I'm going to make sure all of us are on the winning team. See, the Rodrigos will be damn grateful somebody was here to save the night for them. They'll play ball with me, or they'll know what war really is."

Or so Stiles was hoping. It was a long shot, of course. A bunch of mean gringos in an outlaw biker club, teaming up with the Rodrigos, especially now that the Mafia was looking to link up with the new Cali players. Whatever, Stiles figured all it took would be to show no fear, stand up to the little greasers and make them his offer of partnership. If the Mafia didn't like it, wanted to get tough, then he'd take care of them. Either way, he would have enough coke to peddle, clear to California. But the biker leader was looking toward the future, not a one-shot deal.

"Two miles from this spot you showed me on the map?" Stiles asked Miniguez.

"Yes. Once again, I sense you're having trouble believing me."

"We're holding the guns, Carlos. I'm a believer. I lived in these parts most of my life, when I wasn't inside the joint. There's plenty of back roads, in and out of here. As far as I know, anything could go wrong from any direction."

The dealer's voice took on an angry edge. "I'd hope by now, since it is clear my own life is at stake, that you'd trust me. I've already told you, I was at the meeting with my gang when this was arranged by the traitor in the Rodrigo organization. It's happening tonight."

"So, let's do it," Stiles said, then cut a mean smile. "It'll be the first white Christmas, a little early maybe, that I've ever seen in Florida."

A moment later, night-vision goggles were passed out, then each outlaw took a large satchel. The bricks would be stuffed into the bags and would have to be hauled back to the vans on foot. According to the informant inside the Rodrigo organization, there was a little over twelve hundred pounds of cocaine coming in. That much dope would be inspiration enough to forget about the grueling chore of legging it back through the woods.

Slipping on his goggles, the night illuminated in green all around him, Stiles led his outlaw force into the brush.

IN LESS THAN twelve hours, Paul Tartaglia suddenly found himself in a living nightmare. Seated behind his desk in the massive study at his Palm Beach estate, the Don seethed in silence, wondering how to proceed. What was happening all around him was unbelievable. Someone had declared war on him. But who? In order to strike back, he had to put a face on the enemy. Reasons for this sudden assault on his empire could come later, when he had the guy, or guys, hanging from a meat hook and was skinning them alive. Personally.

Indeed, it had been the worst, most terrifying, alarming day of his life.

First, the hit at the beach where he'd lost two top distributors and three soldiers. One second he's standing there, talking business, and the next thing he knew he was being spattered in blood and brains. The fact that he wasn't dropped by a silent bullet told him he had been spared by the sniper, on purpose. But why? Was the hit a message, a warning? Of course he had enemies, but that just went with the territory. Sometimes, he knew who his enemies were. Other times they came at him from the shadows, or maybe smiled to his face while plotting behind his back. Those kind of guys were long gone, washed out to the bottom of the sea, or hacked up and fed to the gators in the Everglades. All this while Paul Tartaglia was still alive and well in Miami, still larger than life, still smoking his Havanas, still moving more coke than half the Cali Cartel. The reason was real simple. Paul Tartaglia had always rooted out his enemies and shown no mercy.

But this was something different. This looked like all-out war, something new and alien to him that was meant to crush him completely. Sure, there was always the crazy Colombians, looking to eliminate competition, honing their blades behind a man's back while sniffing out a weakness, where they could strike. Tartaglia was definitely at the top of the trade, always a prime target for new blood looking to make a name for themselves. Well, if somebody thought that he had grown soft and vulnerable as he closed in on his golden years, he'd surprise them. Don Paolo could still field an army of a hundred soldiers tomorrow and burn down half of South Florida, if that's what it took.

Only now it wasn't that simple. A war took planning, and the cops were now alert to the possibility of shooting between various organizations in Miami who controlled the flow of narcotics into South Florida.

Pure terror had already been hurled in his face, hours ago. First by the sniper who was no doubt a pro. Then followed caution and paranoia, that squirming in his belly when the cops had come swarming all over the beach, hauling him in for questioning. He was grilled by cops who knew what and who he was but until then hadn't been able to prove a damn thing.

He'd called in his team of lawyers, circling all the

legal wagons his millions could buy, when it was obvious the cops were going to try to make him sweat. Since he wasn't being accused of any crime, the police had been forced to let him go. That alone presented yet another obstacle. Tomorrow held the multiplying threat of more phone taps, surveillance, maybe a shakedown of some dealer a little lower on the chain. Hell, his every move might be dogged by plainclothes detectives. At the moment, there was more damage control going on than he'd ever had to face in twenty years of his reign. He was being hit from all directions, and he didn't have a god-damn clue what the hell was going on.

But the day had turned even worse. On top of the beachfront hit, his warehouse down by the river had been stormed by a commando-like strike, by either some unknown enemy, or the DEA, he wasn't sure. Luckily, the warehouse was leased to a legitimate citrus wholesaler, and no one who had gone down in the bloody debacle could be linked directly to him. All he knew was that a load of coke had been blown up, his police source in the department had informed him, by some guy with a bazooka. There was no word who the guy was. But shooting first and asking questions later, especially with a ba-zooka, wasn't standard DEA procedure. No, some-thing else was happening, and it didn't stop at the warehouse.

Only a little while ago, his posh strip club had been hit by somebody, one lone bastard, according to his men, who left the place totaled and under siege by still more cops. Some big guy with a gun had bulldozed his way into the place, rousted one of the managers there, then blasted his way out with a hand cannon, taking with him over a hundred grand in both cash and coke. More dead soldiers at another place of business, with still more cops to deal with, and more lawyers scrambling all over Miami to handle the cops.

Still too many questions with no answers. Well, he had his own sources, his own snitches who owed him. It was time to call in their markers, find out what the hell was happening. Tomorrow, he was meeting with the Rodrigo brothers, all set to nail down one of the biggest shipments of narcotics ever smuggled into Florida. All that was left to do was get the brothers their money. It was hit or miss time, and Tartaglia wasn't going to miss out on this deal.

Now this triple fiasco, with some maniac out there pissing all over his dreams. Not even the Don and all his money could accurately assess all the legal and business fallout of the day's hellish events.

He needed answers, starting now.

It seemed like an eternity had passed before him in the thirty minutes he had sat with one of his top lieutenants, waiting for the ex-football player to get there. Tartaglia saw Michael Palazzi glance at his watch for what seemed like the hundred-and-first time.

''Our guys already picked him, you said?''

Palazzi nodded. ''He called Majors from a pay phone. Majors called me, and I sent Pete and Bruno out. They were already downtown on some business. That was an hour ago. Apparently our football hero's scared to death, what with all the cops crawling all over the place. Pete talked to him, called me back, said he sounds set to wet himself. They ought to be dragging our little playboy in here any minute.''

Don Paolo fired up a foot-long Havana cigar with a gold lighter. ''Something smells here, Michael. I mean, what happened at the club was some kind of cowboy hit, but by who? And why did this guy just let Mathers go, huh? Probably, I'd bet you, without even a scratch on him.''

''I understand what you're saying. But the guy's an ex-football star, Don Paolo. He likes the easy life and all that glitters with it. He's not going to risk pissing all that away to be part of some heist.''

''I'm not so sure. It's public knowledge the guy's had more than his share of problems, both with the dope and money. Who knows what his situation or thinking is? I never cared too much for the idea of Majors bringing him onboard, but the guy was starstruck, loves to have his football heroes around him. When I talk to Majors, you better believe I want him to understand that from now on we keep it tight. No more hot-shit football celebs, just straight shooters who are all business.''

Don Paolo fell grimly silent.

''You want a drink?''

''Damn right. Make it a double whiskey,'' Tartaglia said. As Palazzi went to the wet bar to build two drinks, the Don started thinking out loud. ''We got three separate incidents in one day. One we know for sure was done by a lone man, another we're not sure if it was one guy or a bunch, since the DEA was storming the place, then the hit on the beach.''

"All three related somehow, yeah, sure looks that way. You don't think New York is all of a sudden unhappy with us, do you?''

"After all these years? How about the respect they showed my father? And all the business I've sent their way?'' Tartaglia said, shaking his head in disbelief.

"New York's had a lot of trouble the past few years with the Feds. All the guys rolling up there, throwing themselves into Witness Protection Programs, writing books and making millions while they rat out their bosses. I'm just saying it's another angle we might want to look into. Maybe somebody in New York figures we've had it too good for too long.''

The Don didn't want to even consider the Five Families might move in on his domain, but anything was possible.

The phone rang and Palazzi answered it. Tartaglia took his drink and killed half the whiskey in one gulp as he heard Palazzi growl into the receiver, "Yeah. Okay, bring him in.''

Palazzi went to the wet bar with his drink. "Sounds like you've already made your mind up about the playboy football star.''

"I want to hear him out first.'' Tartaglia showed his right-hand man a cold smile. "Besides, I've never met a football star before.''

The double doors opened and Tartaglia watched

two of his soldiers waltz Ricky Mathers straight toward his desk. The man was sweaty and disheveled, Don Paolo noted. The guy was a little on the skinny side and didn't look like much, not what Tartaglia expected a guy in the NFL to look like.

"You find him alone?" the Don asked Bruno Sartaro.

Sartaro told Tartaglia they found Mathers by himself at a pay phone on a street corner downtown.

"Anybody else know you're here, Ricky?"

Mathers shook his head, appearing startled that the Don addressed him by his first name. "No, sir, Mr. Tartaglia. I took a cab back from where that bastard dumped me off. I called Johnny right away to get in touch with you. Jesus, it was crazy. I mean I'd never seen anything like it."

"All right, calm down. You want a drink, Ricky?"

"Yes, sir, I could use one. That would be very generous of you, Mr. Tartaglia."

The guy was sniveling, dying to be ingratiating, and Don Paolo found himself loathing the mere presence of this so-called sports hero. Damn right, his mind was already made up. This playboy had never gotten his hands dirty or bloody in his whole life, a life where the whole world had dropped itself into his lap because he was a football player. Only in America.

"Have a seat, Ricky. Michael, get Ricky whatever he's drinking."

"Whiskey, straight. Thanks."

"Let's have it."

"I don't know what to tell you, sir."

"Well, you were there. Tell me what happened. Describe the guy who blew my place all to hell and killed my men, good men. And I don't think I need to inform you, Ricky, that club will be out of business for some time. Plus the other two clubs I have will probably be watched by so many undercover cops that it could be months, if ever, before I can even set foot inside, much less conduct any business. I'm a busy man with many problems. So, I want to hear it. Give me the short and the ugly, and don't leave anything out."

Mathers looked nervously at the three mobsters. He took his drink and Don Paolo waited while he gulped it down, getting himself composed. Tartaglia listened to Mathers as he described what had happened.

Mathers's version was about as short and ugly as it could get, Tartaglia decided. It didn't tell him much. Still, the Don was getting a picture of this shooter with the elephant-size balls. He knew they were dealing with a pro, and they suspected it was somebody ex-military, maybe CIA. Definitely a man who'd seen plenty of death and dished out far more than he'd taken, because he was still walking around. There were men like that in the world. They could kick some serious ass, walk on, rack up the experience and use the hell in their hearts to make themselves even stronger than ever. This enemy was like his father, and they were rare and they were special, but Don Paolo hadn't made it that far by underestimating the opposition.

"He, uh, told me to tell you this. I'm sorry, sir, these aren't my words."

"I'm listening," Tartaglia urged.

Clearly, Mathers was uncomfortable delivering the message, since he started breathing heavy and swallowing hard. "Before he let me go, he said, 'Don Paolo has twenty-four hours to dismantle his...cocaine empire and turn himself over to the DEA or...the Grim Reaper will visit him in the dead of night.' And he said 'White Christmas in Miami is over.'"

Tartaglia heard the blood roar into his ears. Rage erupted from deep in his belly, wanting to blow his heart right out of his chest. Somehow he restrained himself from leaping over the desk and ripping this football player apart, limb by limb.

"I'm sorry, Mr. Tartaglia, I really am. I don't know what to make of this, I mean it's insane. I'd never seen this guy in my life. Oh, but I got the make and license number of his car."

Tartaglia wanted to murder someone so bad, he barely heard the ex-football player's mumblings.

"We can check it, but I don't know if anything will come of it," Palazzi said. "Probably a rental, an alias, even stolen credit cards. It could be a stolen vehicle."

Tartaglia puffed on his cigar and stared at nothing for long moments. The Don had a lot to think about, a lot to do before the next day's meet with the Rodrigo brothers. It was beyond Tartaglia, who had never met Mathers before this night, what Majors had ever seen in this guy. It only reaffirmed to Tartaglia that he needed to pay closer attention to all of his businesses from then on, had to even have some personal say in who was hired. He told the two soldiers to take Ricky out front and wait for Palazzi to join them.

When they were alone, Tartaglia told his lieutenant, "Whoever this guy is, he's still in Miami. I want him found and brought before me by tomorrow night. I want this guy begging for his life as I cut him up, piece by piece. Are we clear on that?"

Solemn, Palazzi nodded. "And Johnny's boy wonder?"

"He's a piece of shit. Take him somewhere far outside town, maybe someplace near the Everglades. Work on him, find out if he's told us everything. Then make sure the body never gets found."

6

In less than forty-eight hours, the DEA would be back on-line in their operations against the Tartaglia-Rodrigo connection. Agent Tasker pledged his cooperation with Bolan and Grimaldi but only up to a certain point. From his command center at the hotel suite, the DEA special agent in charge could run and monitor other field operations against the Tartaglias, gather more intel on the Rodrigo connection, grill his star snitch and check out leads. But if Bolan or Grimaldi were picked up by the police, the man said they were on their own. Of course, Brognola could flex muscle and get the two soldiers back on track, but that would prove very time consuming, haggling with the local law. With that in mind, Bolan knew they had to pick up the pace. From there on out it would be extreme hit-and-run, search-and-destroy, snatch-and-grab.

Right now it was time to shut down a major drug factory, a chop-and-step setup the Don ran out of an industrial park in Miami, west of the Palmetto Expressway. Getting in would be the big hurdle alone, but that could prove the least of their problems.

The great danger on this hit-and-run was explained to Bolan during the hour-long interrogation of Artie Fromer. Once the snitch had killed a beer to calm his coke-jittery nerves, he got busy squealing.

Fromer had laid out names, addresses, and what he vowed were the keys to the largest of the Tartaglia drug operations. The snitch had also made a list, and Bolan put his stops in order of priority. According to Fromer, the warehouse was a front that packed and shipped industrial machinery by day. But by night, a large crew of chemists, surrounded by Tartaglia guards carrying assault-rifles, worked underground in a soundproof laboratory to enhance the drugs and stretch their dollar value or turn bricks of powder cocaine into crack. Fromer said he had been there several times to pick up large quantities of cocaine. At any one time, there was as much as two tons of the drug stored below ground. There was also, he said, maybe five hundred to a thousand pounds of heroin. Every night at least a dozen chemists worked on perfecting a smokable rock form of heroin in this vault of sorcery. The problem was the laboratory was chock-full of ether, acetone and kerosene. Fromer believed the Don also shipped chemicals that were necessary to produce cocaine powder in South America. But the chemists were also hard at work, cooking heroin, looking for that magic ingredient that would produce the new misery rock of ages. A firefight in that kind of setup could plaster Bolan, Grimaldi and enemies alike clear to skyscrapers in downtown Miami.

Tricky, all right. But hope was running hard in

Bolan's heart. Hope was called forty pounds of C-4 plastique.

They ditched Grimaldi's black four-door sedan rental near a shack in an abandoned weed-choked lot. One look at the sprawling warehouse in the distance, and Bolan knew it would be a formidable task to get safely inside. At least Fromer said there would be no one on the grounds other than Tartaglia drug people. In this situation, the soldier considered everyone fair game, both gunmen and chemists laboring to further poison America.

If Bolan and Grimaldi pulled off what they had in mind, it would be a major coup, a truly devastating blow to the Tartaglia drug empire.

Both men donned combat blacksuits for the midnight hit. They quickly attached webbing and put twenty pounds of the plastic explosives in their pouches. Bolan cracked a clip into an Uzi submachine gun while Grimaldi cocked and locked his M-16. Spare clips for the automatic weapons went into pouches on their web belts. The Executioner also toted the Beretta with attached sound suppressor, as well as the Desert Eagle, while Grimaldi carried a hip-holstered 9 mm Glock pistol. The soldiers set off for the night watchman.

Crouching, they darted across a short stretch of no-man's-land, taking cover behind a trash bin. Beyond the chain-link fence, Bolan figured they'd have to run another twenty yards to the back door. Two 18-wheelers and several luxury vehicles sat, dark and empty, near the loading docks. They found no one around the perimeter of the warehouse. The place looked shut down. That, of course, was the intended illusion.

Bolan found the watchman, smoking a cigarette, his back turned to them. The man was alone, outside the booth. Fromer had informed them there was only one man on duty. Slinging the Uzi and drawing the Beretta, the Executioner broke cover, Grimaldi right on his heels. The watchman was a fraction of a second too late in reacting to the sudden dash of two armed men. As he reached for a holstered .357 Magnum revolver, Bolan swept over him, thrusting the Beretta in his face.

"Who the hell are you? What do you want?"

"Special delivery. We need to get into the building," Bolan growled.

"You're crazy."

"Maybe. You want to find out just how crazy?"

Bolan took the revolver and tucked it in his waistband. He locked an arm around the man's throat and hauled him toward the back door.

"You know who owns this place, pal?" the watchman rasped.

When they got to the steel door, Bolan ordered, "Open it. Try to scream, get cute, I'll take you off Don Paolo's payroll permanently."

Grimaldi covered their rear as the watchman keyed open the door. Bolan clipped the guy over the head with the Beretta, then took his handcuffs and secured the man's hands behind his back. After dragging the guard out of sight, laying him behind a parked Cadillac, the soldier moved back to the doorway. Cautious, Beretta poised to fire, Bolan

slipped through the opening. Quietly, Grimaldi shut
the door behind them. They were unfamiliar with
the layout, but Fromer had said there were two large
hatches in the floor at the north end. Maybe four
gunmen were upstairs in a storeroom, with usually
another four with automatic weapons below to mind
the shop. Fromer believed there was a silent alarm
under a desk in the north room, but he wasn't sure.

The Executioner found himself in a narrow hallway. He saw a light and heard a voice muttering
from somewhere. He was nearing the end of the hall
when a figure with an assault rifle whirled around
the corner.

Bolan beat the guy to the finish by a millisecond.
The Beretta shot one 9 mm slug through the gunner's forehead. But as the hardman went down, his
dying reflex triggered a short burst of autofire.

Surging on, the Executioner rounded the corner.
Gunfire came in two directions from a large room
that looked more like an office than a storehouse.
Darting for cover behind a large desk, with Grimaldi
peeling off to his flank, Bolan picked out two targets. With the wall tattooed behind him with whiz-
zing slugs, Bolan popped up from the desk. One pull
of the Beretta's trigger sent the guy with an M-16
flying into a stack of crates, a neat red hole in his
chest. His flaming assault rifle continued spraying
aimless rounds toward the ceiling. Tracking on, the
next 9 mm round burst from the Executioner's Beretta and cored through his new opponent's eye.

Bolan needed a live one to get them into the underground lab. He drew target acquisition on a big

guy surging toward a desk. The hardman was reaching under the desk, going for an alarm, Bolan assumed, when the Executioner pumped two slugs into his arm. He cried out in pain, clutched his arm and went down. Autofire chattered on his flank, and Bolan saw Grimaldi scythe down two more goons with automatic weapons. The big room then appeared empty to Bolan. Turning, he saw the wounded hardman scrambling to reach the desk.

Like an Olympic hurdler, Bolan vaulted the desk, watching the man's finger reaching for a button.

HE HADN'T GIVEN himself the nickname ''Judas'' on a whim. Ben Stiles would just as soon cut a man's throat in an act of treachery to get what he wanted than look at the intended victim. Many times he had turned on guys who considered him a pal, an associate in crime, or even a drinking buddy if he just didn't like the guy. More than once he had seized the reins of power in a circle of drug dealers or car thieves by setting up the guy who thought he was in charge, then plunging a blade into his back. In the world he lived in, only the strongest, the meanest, and the quickest survived. Naturally, he demanded loyalty at all times, and if he ever thought there was even a flicker of some conspiracy in a man's eyes, he'd kill that man instantly. Rule by fear. It's the law of the jungle.

So Stiles found himself in tune to this setup with the Colombian. Treachery often cleaned house, got rid of the vulnerable links in a chain, the way Stiles saw it. Betrayal was okay, he thought, as long as he was the one doing it.

Right now it was time to clean house of some Cali deadweight.

Waiting with his men at the south edge of the woods, the biker leader stared across the drop site. They had been waiting there a good hour, but Stiles saw at least eight figures with automatic weapons across the field. Two vans were parked nearby. The field looked big enough to land a Learjet, but Stiles suspected the aircraft would just fly low over the site and dump its cargo on the fly.

Fifteen minutes later, the Learjet appeared and did just that. It came in low, angling for the lone flare one of the shadows had just set. Its lights flashed on as the aircraft cleared the trees. As it streaked over the field, three bales were pushed from a large doorway on the portside, dropped from twenty feet up. The bundles hit the soft earth, bounced hard but didn't seem to break on impact, no doubt the product cushioned with something, maybe hay, Stiles figured.

Miniguez informed Stiles the hit team would come from the north. When the Rodrigo crew scrambled for the bales, Stiles then discovered Miniguez had so far proved himself a reliable source of information. How the Rodrigo crew had missed the gunmen waiting to pounce on them, Stiles didn't know. But he guessed the Cali hit crew had concealed themselves in the dense brush to the north and remained still as stone.

The rival Cali gang came out, firing with automatic weapons. Rodrigo gunmen returned fire, but they were caught off guard by the lightning strike. Still, the brothers' hardforce poured it on, cutting down a few of the hitters who maybe numbered ten in all, just like Miniguez said.

"Grab our boy, Brewer," Stiles growled at a giant biker with a shaved skull, nodding at Miniguez.

Then Stiles led the charge across the field. In perfect unison, the Devil's Horsemen cut loose with autofire. They mowed down everything that moved with leaden walls of their savage weapons, sweeping the drug runners, flank to flank. It helped that the Rodrigos had nearly gone down to a man against the rival crew, and had managed to decimate the strike force by half. It was so easy, Stiles wanted to laugh out loud.

But it wasn't over yet. Hideous groans of pain echoed across the field from wounded men. The Devil's Horsemen swept over the dying and pumped short bursts of autofire into their chests.

One swarthy and badly bleeding figure mumbled at Stiles, but in Spanish.

"What did he say?" Stiles growled at Miniguez.

"He cursed you in reference to your mother's private parts."

Stiles chuckled. "Well, translate this. Tell him that wasn't very nice. And ask him if he knows it's illegal to sell narcotics in this country." Miniguez balked and Stiles snapped, "Do it. I'm not joking."

Miniguez translated the message in Spanish, then just as the wounded drug runner started to curse in his native tongue again, Stiles held back the trigger on his M-16 and turned the guy's face into pulp.

The biker leader looked around and found his men already cutting open the bales with their knives, loading their satchels. Stiles gave his pack to Miniguez and ordered, "You can have the honors, amigo."

THE EXECUTIONER KICKED the man in the chest just as his finger reached for the button. The guy hit the floor hard on his back, grabbing at his new source of pain. A quick sweep of the storeroom and Bolan found the three of them were alone. Grimaldi kept vigilance just the same with his M-16. No movement, no sound other than the hardman growling curses at Bolan's feet.

The soldier yanked the gunman to his feet. "Get us below."

"I don't know who you crazy bastards are, but you go down there and start spraying the place in a wild-ass tear, you'll blow us all clear out to the bay."

"Just get us to the hatch," Bolan rasped, spinning the guy and planting the muzzle of the Uzi in his ear.

"You're dead men. You'll never get out of here alive."

The Executioner shoved the gunman away. The guy scowled but led them to the far corner of the room. There, he rolled back a desk on wheels. Bolan took the key to the hatch, then rapped the Uzi across the hardman's jaw, sending him reeling backward, landing in a sprawled heap on top of the desk.

Bolan looked at Grimaldi. It was going to be dicey once they plunged below. They'd have to move fast and hope the Don's soldiers were more interested in saving the dope than starting a gunfight.

The soldier slipped the Uzi across his shoulder and drew the Beretta, wanting to control the situation without having to resort to bursts of autofire. Grimaldi fisted his Glock, hanging the M-16 from his shoulder.

Bolan lifted the hatch, the Beretta aimed down. Bright light showed at the bottom of a short flight of steps, but no figures. He caught the faint sounds of some scuffling from somewhere, then descended the steps. Halfway down, he stuck a baseball-sized glob of plastique under the steps. All the C-4 blocks were primed with detonators homed into the same frequency of the remote-control radio box in the sedan's trunk.

The soldier reached the bottom of the steps. He found a huge room, and just as Fromer had said. Ten guys in filter masks, white smocks and gloves were spread around long tables with trays of white powder. Tubes, vials and burners were scattered around the tables. All over the room, pallets were heaped with countless white bricks. And in the far corner Bolan saw the fifty-five-gallon drums, stacked neatly. No one seemed to notice the two invaders, not even the four men with assault rifles that Bolan found strolling around the chemists.

That changed in the next heartbeat.

A pair of eyes over a filter mask spotted Bolan and Grimaldi, the weapons in their hands. Those eyes were bulging in terror next, the chemist throwing his hands up. His voice was muffled by the mask as he shouted, "Don't shoot, no shooting! You'll blow us all to kingdom come!"

The hardmen whirled toward Bolan and Grimaldi, their weapons tracking the two invaders. The two soldiers split up at the end of a long table.

"Drop the weapons!" Bolan snarled.

"Fuck you!" a hardman shouted.

"No!" a chemist screamed.

It was an eyeblink away from going bad, but the hardmen checked their fire. Bolan saw the guards were far enough away from the drums of chemicals to risk it. If the standoff cracked and all hell broke loose, it was over for everybody.

Bolan started to trigger the Beretta. Grimaldi had been with the Executioner on so many hellfire campaigns that he'd already anticipated the only play that could save them both from certain doom. One by one, the two soldiers dropped the gunmen with deadly precise head shots. Chemists screamed, but they were rooted in pure terror where they stood. As the hardmen dropped, one dead goon triggered a short burst from his Heckler & Koch MP-5 submachine gun. Bolan braced himself for the inevitable worst.

But the wild line of autofire marched across a chemist's chest, his white smock turned to sudden crimson, his twitching body absorbing the lead before he toppled, facedown, in a tray of white powder.

"Everyone stay where you are," the Executioner ordered.

They kept their hands high in the air. Bolan took two filter masks from a table and tossed one to Grimaldi. The place reeked with the pungent odor of chemicals, the air around the tables shrouded by thin white veils. Mask on, Bolan kept his vigilance up as the two men went to work planting the C-4 around the lab.

When he was done, Bolan addressed the chemists. "All of you can consider yourselves fired. I suggest you get as far away from here as fast as you can."

They didn't have to be told twice. Bolan and Grimaldi followed the stampede up the stairs.

WITH GRIMALDI BEHIND the sedan's wheel, the Executioner watched the pandemonium in the lot as his friend raced them down a narrow paved road that led north from the warehouse. Men were running like crazy, tire rubber screeching, vehicles scrambling out of there. Even the cuffed watchman was racing past the booth, as voices shouted from all directions.

"You want the honors, or you want me to do it?" Bolan asked Grimaldi.

"I'll let you set off the fireworks, but give me a second so I can get into position to watch the show."

Grimaldi braked the sedan. As the ace pilot turned his head, the Executioner thumbed the switch.

There was a rumbling of seismic force beneath the sedan's wheels, then Bolan saw the entire warehouse uprooted in a titanic blinding fireball. A series of follow-up explosions seemed to have even more force, taking on an even greater brilliance as the chemicals in the lab ignited. At some point just beyond the blast, Bolan glimpsed thin curtains of white powder raining over the lot.

Grimaldi showed his friend a grim smile. "Who said it couldn't snow in South Florida?"

7

The night was far from over. In fact, as far as Bolan was concerned, the nightmare had only begun for Paul Tartaglia.

Bolan figured he and Grimaldi had already inflicted hurricane-like damage on the Don's empire, but with all the businesses Tartaglia owned and all the contacts and connections he had in the drug underworld, the soldier knew the two of them were moving through a shadowy maze, barely scratching the surface. Each new lead, every fresh angle could steer them straight into another pool of human sharks. From his grim, and more often than not savage, experience in dealing with major criminals, Bolan knew that the cannibals, especially in the drug trade, knew of or about one another. Dealers and wholesalers kept their ears close to the ground at all times, either watching their stashes or plotting the expansion of turf. In short, guys talked in the trade, always in code, ever paranoid, but everyone knew what the other guy was doing. And for damn sure word would spread like wildfire through Miami about Tartaglia's current and very disastrous situation. The soldier's one fleeting regret was that he couldn't be on hand when the Don heard about his lab and all his dope going up in a fireball. The rare indulgence was short-lived because the night was going to turn even uglier, Bolan strongly suspected.

The next stop for the two men was a posh estate in Coconut Grove. It was time to shake down a top counsel for the Don. The lawyer's name was Matt Parker, late-thirties, defense attorney for the Family, according to Fromer, although the snitch wasn't quite sure if Parker even practiced law anymore. Fromer also claimed that not only did the playboy counsel like his late-night parties, but he moved a few keys out of his bayfront estate for the Family. Since the snitch had been there to party with the Family counsel on more than one occasion, Bolan was running with the lead. And what the soldier needed was hard intel on the connection between Tartaglia and the Rodrigos. Fromer said that Parker almost always sat in on any major deal that went down with the Family, and helped work out the logistics of moving the dope to other states through the Don's legitimate companies in other parts of the country. It stood to reason that Matt Parker knew enough about Don Paolo's business to make Tartaglia burn with regret and fury in the next day or so.

Bolan knew he could go straight for the Don's head anytime. He could have taken the Miami godfather out on the beach with the opening shot of the campaign. But Bolan's plan was to gather all the vipers in one nest and trample them all underfoot. If one member of the Family or the Rodrigos was left standing, in six months' time it would be back to business as usual. And the word from Fromer was that one of the largest shipments of narcotics ever was being brought into the country soon. The Executioner intended to be on hand when the deal went down.

Naturally, Tartaglia and the Rodrigos would be on full alert, more cautious and paranoid than ever. In a way that could work to Bolan's advantage. If the traffickers felt the noose tightening, they might well attempt to speed up their timetable for the deal. Maybe. And the Don's sick brother, dying from some mysterious illness? Bolan hadn't made a decision either way about Sal Tartaglia. But he'd be up to visiting the man, in time, depending on how the campaign fell.

"This good enough, Sarge?"

Bolan looked at the secluded back road that ended in some dense brush. They had already passed and marked the lawyer's estate. The soldier had counted at least six vehicles in the circular drive but with all the lush vegetation, especially the palm trees that hid most of the estate from view, it was difficult to tell how many people were with the Family lawyer.

"We'll leg it in from here. According to the snitch, our mark doesn't go in for electric fences, hidden cameras or motion detectors. Should be a straight walk-in for us."

"You trust Fromer?"

"Like I would a cobra. But he's dealing for his life, so we run with it. Any unforeseen problems we have, believe me, I'll go straight to him for an accounting."

"Good enough for me."

After Grimaldi slid the sedan deep into the brush, the two men were out, ready and on the move in less than a minute.

This time around, Bolan and Grimaldi donned black ski masks. Custom-made sound suppressors were attached to Bolan's Beretta and Grimaldi's Glock. Just in case it went south, they had their automatic weapons slung around their shoulders. Fromer had indicated that Parker kept an armed security force on hand, three hardmen of the Tartaglia Family to be exact. The gunners had to go, of course, quick and final. Grimaldi knew the drill. Everyone would be rounded up, forced on the floor, tied up with whatever was available. On the surface it would look like a standard home invasion, which was why Bolan had the large nylon sack hung around his shoulders.

Together, the two men swiftly moved up the narrow stretch of sand along the bay. North, the lights of Miami and Miami Beach burned in the night.

Shortly, they made their way through a jungle of vegetation. In the distance, Bolan caught the sounds of someone splashing in the pool, a woman laughing. Moments later, the whitewashed estate loomed in Bolan's sight. A naked woman hopped out of the pool, dried herself off and wrapped the towel around her nubile tanned frame before moving through a sliding door that she'd left open.

Bolan and Grimaldi scaled the six-foot wall and landed on the concrete deck, side by side, with catlike grace. It was a big place, two stories, and Bolan couldn't even guess how many rooms were in the estate. It would be too time-consuming to check each and every room, but Fromer indicated the party was always confined to the main living room. Apparently, Parker liked to keep everyone in sight.

Beretta out, Bolan was moving up the backside of the estate, toward the sliding doors, when two figures appeared. Silently, the Executioner slipped behind a palm tree, Grimaldi falling in behind him. Peering around the edge of the tree, Bolan spotted two big men in aloha shirts, each with a shoulder-holstered .357 Magnum revolver. They fired up cigarettes.

"How about all this shit that's gone down, huh, Freddie? I mean a goddamn war's been declared on us, and the Don's mouthpiece is in there with his bunnies, partying up a frigging storm like there's no tomorrow. Tell you what. I ought to march right in there and slap him."

Freddie was staring at the bay, as if searching for something. "Yeah, I don't like it one bit myself, but what are you going to do? He's the fair-haired boy and all, with the keys to the kingdom. Don treats him with too much respect, go figure. Maybe he sees something in Parker. Maybe the son he lost? All this, while the Don's sweating out the night, ready to nail down the deal of the century with the brothers tomorrow."

"Give it one hour, then I end the party. It's getting late, and the boss needs our party boy there with him in the morning."

It was just the break Bolan was looking for. Parker would be at the meet. Bolan needed to have a heart-to-heart with the lawyer about the man's future.

The Executioner made his move. He whirled around the tree, triggered the Beretta twice. A one-two punch of quiet lead drilled through the skulls of the hardmen. They toppled to the ground.

In tandem, Bolan and Grimaldi were through the door, weapons leveled on the party group. The two invaders in black ski masks got everyone's instant and undivided attention. Unfortunately, a brunette started to scream.

Striding into the large living room, Bolan spotted two gunmen wheel through a coral archway to his left flank, but the two soldiers were ready for the sudden threat. Enemy revolvers were out and tracking the invaders, but they were a heartbeat too slow. Bolan's Beretta and Grimaldi's Glock pumped two shots into the gunmen. The gunners slammed into the archway, crumpled, their shattered skulls leaking blood and brain matter on the white-tiled floor.

Alert for movement from any direction around the living room, Bolan reached the marble coffee table, grabbed the brunette by the hair and hauled her to her feet. He didn't intend to shoot the woman, of course. Instead, he hoped that when he jammed the Beretta in her face it would cut off her screams. It worked.

The soldier counted four women and two men, spread out along the plush white couch. Cocaine, both powder and rock, was heaped on the coffee table along with other drug paraphernalia. Behind

Bolan, Grimaldi dragged the two hardmen from the pool deck into the living room.

"Everyone do as they're told, don't scream, don't fight us, and no one gets hurt." Bolan sought out the lean, handsome face he believed was Parker. "You Parker?"

A shaky nod. "Who are you? What do you want?"

"Whatever's in your safe, and you better not disappoint me. Is there anyone else in the house?"

Parker shook his head.

"You better be telling me the truth, or everyone here gets one in the head, you understand?"

"There's no one here. If you've come to rob me, I'll get what I have for you, then leave. But for God's sake, don't kill anyone!"

Bolan flung the woman onto the couch, grabbed Parker by the front of his silk robe and hauled him to his feet. The Executioner gave Grimaldi a nod.

"Everyone out into the middle of the floor, facedown," the Stony Man pilot barked. "Now!"

"Where?" Bolan snarled in the lawyer's ear, the Beretta jammed in the base of Parker's skull.

"Upstairs, in the bedroom."

At the moment, it appeared just what Bolan and Grimaldi wanted it to look like. A robbery. But when Bolan had the lawyer alone, he was going to put the facts of life to the man, and in no uncertain terms. It would be up to the lawyer whether he made that meet with the Rodrigos the next day.

As Bolan trailed Parker up the winding white stone steps, he glanced sideways. Grimaldi had everyone on the floor. So far the fort was being held down. But Bolan knew anything could go wrong. He'd better move fast.

WHEN THEY THUNDERED into their compound, the place came alive. Stiles felt like a conquering hero returning home as he saw some of his men, with M-16s, left behind to guard the compound, rolling out to greet him. The bikers' women stepped through the doorways of the three lodges. More silhouettes appeared from the workshop, sliding past the Harleys, assault rifles in hand.

Stiles ignored everyone's calls of either congratulations or questions of wanting to know if he got it. From there on, he knew he'd have to be careful with that much coke around. Everyone in the compound knew what was going on, but there'd been no other way. He needed everyone pulling for them, or they were gone. Gone meant a bullet through the head and dumped in the swamp.

They killed the engines on their bikes near the main lodge, which Stiles called his command center. The leader swung off the saddle. "Brewer, get all the shit together and inside now. Carlos, you come with me. You've got a call to make."

A skinny redhead swept over to Stiles, kissed him on the mouth, then hugged him. He was so fueled on adrenaline that it took a moment for Stiles to recognize her as his old lady, Peaches. "Everything go down the way you wanted it, baby?"

He pushed her away. "This is business, bitch. Ain't looking to throw some big old snow party."

She frowned and Stiles told her, "Give me some time. You'll get yours."

Stiles made a beeline for their command center. Entering the game room with its pool tables, bar, dartboards and giant screen TV, he looked over his shoulder as his cohorts surged inside behind him. They carried the satchels and still toted the hardware they'd used to nail down this victory. He was searching their faces for some hint of treachery or dangerous greed. They were all wild-eyed with relief and postbattle euphoria, but their laughter was strained and nervous-sounding. They started clapping one another on the backs, grabbing one another up in bearhugs and passing whiskey bottles.

"All right, knock it off." Stiles shouted, "Everyone in the War Room."

Moments later Stiles was in the large room. It was good to be back, but there was still a lot to do. He took in the surroundings as they piled into the room. Here was the one place where he truly felt safe, where he commanded and planned all operations for his Devil's Horsemen.

A wall map of Florida was beyond the conference table, and a banner with their colors hung from floor to ceiling in one corner. Next to their colors was a TV mounted from the ceiling, but it was a long bar heaped with liquor bottles that Stiles went for. There, he uncapped a bottle of whiskey and took a deep gulp to steady his nerves. He told the men to dump the stuff and count all the bricks. It was time-consuming, but he waited, drank and worked out the plan in his head.

It was real simple—have Miniguez make whatever calls were necessary to arrange a meet with the Rodrigos at their home that night, and take twenty bricks, all of which were wrapped in thick orange plastic, obviously the color the Rodrigos used so they could tell which bricks belonged to them. Word would undoubtedly reach the drug-dealing brothers soon enough about their fiasco near the Everglades. In steps, Stiles would explain how he and his Devil's Horsemen were ready to cut themselves in, proving themselves by having helped the Rodrigos save their load from their rivals, which they hadn't seen or prepared for. The Devil's Horsemen were now in the Rodrigo fold, or else he'd declare war on the brothers, hell, he would go gunning for the whole Tartaglia Family if that's what it took. This wasn't a time to back off, Stiles thought. No, they were going for broke, running for the big time.

Finally, it was announced they had exactly six hundred bricks, and some of the bikers whistled.

Stiles went to a safe that was built into the floor. He dialed it open, keeping his back to his men. Only he had the combination, and what was about to go into the vault was his entire future. He opened the safe, then turned and fixed a gaze on Brewer. "Put the stash down the hole. Keep one satchel with twenty bricks. We'll be taking two vans, eight men. Hardware, too."

While they dumped the coke into the vault, Stiles kept searching their faces. This wasn't the time to trust anything on the surface. His gaze narrowed as he looked at Burnout. The short, dumpy biker was a former heavy crank user with wet red eyes that always bulged. Stiles didn't like what he saw on Burnout's face. He had never liked the man much anyway. He was a big mouth who often proved himself a borderline malcontent, with questionable allegiance.

"Something bothering you, Burnout?"

The biker cleared his throat, looked around at his comrades, fidgeting with his hands. "Well, I don't know. I don't like it."

Stiles felt his blood race with anger. A few of the men cursed Burnout. "What don't you like?"

"All this dope you're wanting to deal with the Colombians and the Mafia. I mean, come on, Judas, bro, why risk it? Why not deal this ourselves? We got contacts. We could make a fortune by ourselves."

"Why you little punk," Brewer snarled. "You don't get it, do you? We didn't risk everything for a one-shot deal. This is our ticket to make our club the biggest bunch of one-percenters—"

Stiles cut Brewer off. "Okay, okay." Slowly he started walking toward Burnout. "What are you saying, bro? You want out?"

"No, not really."

"Then what, 'really'?" the leader growled. "You want me to give you a couple of keys, let you ride on, with your old lady, maybe? Go deal yourself?"

"Come on, Judas, you know I'm with you, but I just can't see the point in risking it from here on."

Stiles nodded. So that was the way it was going to be. All right, he decided, it was time to make an example. He went back to the vault. There, he pulled out two bricks, tossed them on the table in front of Burnout.

"Okay, bro, you want to do it your way? Go on, take it and get out."

Burnout looked around at the grim faces. He hesitated, then said, "Look, I'm sorry, but I've waited all my life for a big score like this. I got to have it. I may never get another chance like this."

No one said a word. Angry eyes pinned the biker with contempt and hatred. With a trembling hand, Burnout was reaching for the kilos when Stiles leapt onto the table. He was drawing his knife as Burnout started to backpedal, realizing, too late, what was going to happen. The biker's mouth was open wide but before he could scream, Stiles dropped on him with full force. Burnout slammed to the floor, the boss landing on top of him.

"I don't think so," Stiles rasped, then plunged the blade into the biker's throat, ripped, twisted and pulled the knife free. As he stood, he searched his men's faces. There were a couple of nods and murmurs of approval. It was settled. They were going all the way, or they weren't going at all. The blood from one of their own was on their leader's hands, and it spoke for all of them. If someone else wanted out, they knew the deal.

Stiles pinned the Colombian with a fierce stare. "What are you waiting for? Make the call!"

Stiles slammed the phone on the table as Brewer shoved Miniguez away from the twitching corpse.

PARKER REACHED INTO the wall safe in his bedroom and did exactly what Bolan had braced himself for. The snub-nosed .38 revolver was swinging toward him when the soldier swept over Parker, grabbing his gun hand in a viselike grip. One short right to the counselor's jaw, and Bolan watched the man crumple at his feet. Quickly, tucking the weapon in his waistband, the soldier pulled out three kilos of cocaine, stacks of hundred- and fifty-dollar bills, then took some jewels, just to make it look good.

When he was finished cleaning out the safe and stuffing the sack, Bolan grabbed Parker by the shoulder and tossed the man onto the bed. The Executioner got to the point right away by triggering a 9 mm round that tore a hole in the bed, between Parker's legs. The counselor flinched, his eyes wide in terror. Parker checked himself and looked about to faint with relief.

"We're going to have a talk," Bolan said, aiming the Beretta at the man's crotch. "I need information about the meet tomorrow, and I need to know more about this big shipment. Don't leave anything out or I'll leave you worse than dead."

Something changed in Parker's eyes. He suddenly suspected there was more going on here than a simple robbery. "Who are you?"

"You've heard about all the problems Don Paolo has been having around town today?"

"You? One guy has done all that—"

"You forgot about my friend downstairs. He's lent me a helping hand. We've been everywhere, Parker. It's been a real busy day."

"No kidding. I was watching the news a little while ago. It's a war zone out there. I had to turn it off, it was spooking me so bad."

"Then you must know the Don and the Rodrigos are going down, Parker. And I doubt they'll all be marched off in cuffs by the DEA."

"You're not DEA, are you? No, of course you aren't," the guy blurted, answering his own question.

"Let's just say I'm in Miami to put Tartaglia out of business for good. The clock's ticking, Parker. You've got five seconds to spill your guts, or I'll spill them for you. If you're smart and you're straight with me, you could live through this."

"Okay, okay, I got the picture."

The guy obviously wanted to hold on to his world, but Bolan already had Parker sized as the kind of man who would turn on anyone, even his own, to save himself. So the soldier listened while the lawyer told him he was the Don's top man in controlling the distribution network. When a shipment was expected, everyone was on standby, around-the-clock. Arrangements were already made in advance to get the product moved as quickly as possible out of Florida. New York, Atlanta, New Orleans and Houston were the main cities where the Don had wholesalers who had already paid for the product. Parker made the arrangements to have the timetable worked out, get the paperwork in order for what would look like shipments of citrus.

"How is it moved?" Bolan asked.

"By truck. Straight up I-95. There is one main

trucking company the Don uses for a shipment this size.''

''Where?''

Bolan was told the trucking company was just outside the Miami city limits. The soldier needed to have a look at the trucking company, maybe have a heart-to-heart chat with whoever was in charge there.

''Who runs this place?''

''A guy named Mike Waters,'' Parker answered.

''I need to talk to him. I assume he's also on standby?''

''At a time like this, you bet.'' The lawyer gave Bolan directions to a bar where Waters could probably be found, a dive that stayed open well into the early-morning hours. ''I work close with Waters on the out-of-state shipping. He's the man who could probably tell you more, like the date maybe. The Don stays in close contact with him.''

Bolan asked for a description of Waters, and Parker gave it to him. Gut instinct told the soldier the deal was going to happen fast, especially after the havoc he and Grimaldi had wreaked. He even suspected the load was already in the country.

''How much dope do you think is involved tomorrow?'' the Executioner asked.

''I've talked to the accountant, Rich Bartelli, earlier tonight. Looks like a lot of money has already been wired to overseas accounts. But I hear the Rodrigos want to see a few duffel bags of cold cash tomorrow. As a show of good faith, I guess. I don't know, we're talking somewhere in the two-, maybe three-billion-dollar range for the whole deal. Mostly coke, but we're expecting close to a thousand pounds of heroin in that shipment.''

"All right, here's the deal. You go to the meet. You get your friends downstairs under control, do whatever you have to do to make this look like a straight home invasion, from telling everyone from the cops to the Don. Then make that meet. I'll be in touch tomorrow. If I sense you've screwed me, I'll find you and make you regret the day you were ever born. Are we clear on that?''

The guy nodded but looked away from Bolan. The soldier sensed the man was hiding something.

"What, Parker?''

"Well, I overheard one of the Don's men you wasted downstairs bragging about having somebody inside the DEA on their payroll.''

Bolan felt his heart skip a beat. "You hear any names?''

Parker shook his head. "No. Look, I've come clean with you. This thing has gotten too serious for me. I've been thinking about getting out of this for some time. I just want my life back.''

Bolan stared at the guy, sniveling to save his world, and felt utter contempt. The soldier looked at all the pillows on the bed and told Parker, "Grab every pillowcase you've got. We go downstairs to tie everybody up. Remember, do something stupid and your world ends tonight.''

8

Paul Tartaglia felt like a prisoner in his own home. Given the current crisis, though, he had no choice but to remain on the estate grounds until he got some hard answers about the bastards out there who were giving him more grief than he'd ever believed he could endure in a hundred lifetimes. Better yet, he wanted results, concrete and in blood.

With nothing to do but wait, Don Paolo stayed secluded in his study, his soldiers, inside the mansion and patrolling the grounds, armed to the teeth and on full alert. At this point there was no telling what would happen.

But the Don was handling all phone calls personally.

And he had even been making some calls himself, wasting no time, going for the damage control right away.

Twenty minutes earlier he had called the money-men. Duffel bags were stuffed with hundred-dollar bills, everything in order, ready to go. Were they on for tomorrow? As far as he knew, the Don had told them, it was still set to happen. Be on call, ready to move at a moment's notice.

Then he had called the Rodrigos. The brothers were nervous, but that was understandable. They hadn't asked a lot of questions on the phone, only demanding to know what was going on and were his problems going to become their problems. Tartaglia was told that the brothers had been hit. A load of merchandise had been ripped off by a rival Cali group. No firm details, not over the phone anyway, no accusations, no outbursts of anger. If nothing else, that bit of news cased a nagging fear the Don had that maybe the Rodrigos were the cause of his current nightmare.

Either way, the deal was still on. Good news for a change.

Then the phone rang five minutes after the Don hung up with Fernando Rodrigo. The news the Don received from one of his two DEA sources was both promising and alarming. It seemed the man who wanted to topple his kingdom, an upper-level dealer, Artie Fromer, was caged up by the DEA's Organized Crime Task Force, but in some pretty posh style. Apparently, the guy was singing loud and clear. A problem, but nothing he couldn't handle.

The Don could have sent a hit team over to the hotel suite, but for the moment, it would be wise to put the hit on the backburner. First order of business was to deal with the Rodrigos. A frontal assault on the DEA, wiping out agents all over the place, would bring certain heat down on his head. So he decided to wait until after the load was in hand and on the move out of Florida before sending a hit team after the snitch. No matter what, he had to move quick, cover his tracks, maybe even get every last bit of merchandise he had on hand out of the state as soon as possible. After all, he was looking at close to a hundred-million-dollar deal, and the Rodrigos were expecting a down payment of twenty million in cash the next day.

The deal of the century, damn right. With any luck at all, he could pick up the Rodrigo product tomorrow sometime, and get it trucked to wholesale distribution points in other states. Shipping crews were even then on twenty-four hour standby, ready to load and make the run. It was good in a way the stuff he promised was already paid for by his wholesalers. And it wasn't an understatement, he knew, to say his life was on the line.

So it was the second bit of news from his source that disturbed Tartaglia the most. Apparently, a covert war had been declared on his empire. Two guys, he had been informed, supposedly with the Justice Department, were the ones responsible for all the misery he had suffered. For legitimate government agents to go around Miami, burning down guys, blowing up his places of business, well, it was definitely a new twist on the opposing side's war on drugs. Two guys, cowboys with carte blanche, it seemed. Hell, a license to kill and commit utter mayhem. Unbelievable.

For years the DEA, the Justice Department, every Miami cop, uniformed and plain clothes alike, not in his pocket had hit a stone wall every time they thought they were going to close the net on him. Maybe the government was fed up with operations that were legal and constitutional and had factored in a new way, an edge to beat him. If this ever got to court, Tartaglia's lawyers would have him walking out with no problem, no hassles, even if they found a thousand kilos right in his study. He was supposed to be protected by the law, wasn't he? He had rights like any other citizen, didn't he?

Either way, war had been declared on him, covert or otherwise. And the only solution was to strike back. Their strategy was obvious. He wasn't meant to ever see the inside of a courtroom.

Well, he had descriptions of the two guys, and one of the descriptions fit the human cannon who had erupted through his exclusive club. His soldiers were right now out on the streets, covering his key places of business. If at all possible, they were under explicit orders to bring the two bastards back to him alive.

He poured himself a stiff Scotch whiskey at the wet bar to wait for positive news, right, while he was sweating out the night, on the verge of the biggest deal ever.

He was going back to his desk when the phone rang. His heart started racing with hope of a breakthrough. He picked up the portable, turned it on and said, "Yeah."

It was Eddie, somewhere downtown. The Don caught the fear in Eddie's voice first, then an eternal moment later, he heard Eddie say, "You're not going to believe this. I don't even know how to tell you what's happened."

Tartaglia felt his heart sink. "Just tell me." After all, he thought, how much worse could things get?

The Don dropped into his chair when he heard the news. He heard how their biggest lab was blown up, halfway across town, from the looks of it. He heard how there were fire trucks, cops and news crews. It looked like something out of Beirut, like a car bomb that took out five city blocks. The Don was so stunned he didn't even hear the rest. Then his soldier was asking what he should do next.

Everything was going to hell. Tartaglia felt his life slipping away. He couldn't even begin to comprehend how much dope he had lost, but knew it was somewhere in the two-ton range, could be as much as three tons. That didn't include all the ether, kerosene and acetone he was contracted to move to Colombia. And now all those chemists, scrambling all over Miami, maybe being picked up by the cops.

The Don then began shaking with rage, but kept it out of his voice as he told his soldier, "Do whatever it takes, but I want those two fuckers found before the sun rises. Don't come back here without them."

Tartaglia slammed down the phone so hard it shattered. Then the full weight of the horror struck him, just as badly as a bullet would have shattered a knee or an elbow. The rage exploded from deep in his belly and seemed to give him superhuman strength as he grabbed the underside of his desk. Cursing at the top of his lungs, he lifted the desk and sent it crashing to the floor. He wasn't even aware his soldiers had burst into the study. He was locked in a red world of utter rage as he stormed to the bar, grabbed a bottle and hurled it across the room. Right before the bottle hit the mirror, he caught a glimpse of his face twisted in the insanity of his murderous fury. Someone was going to pay the price for his nightmare.

ASTRIDE HIS HARLEY, Stiles waited while the electronic wrought-iron gates opened. He hit the throttle and led his men along the road to the house. It was time to play it out for all it was worth. He gunned the engine again, making sure his arrival was announced. He was a frigging hero, after all. Why not show off a little to these drug-dealing greaseballs who thought they were more above the law than anybody else?

For a moment, he sat, smiling at all the guys with holstered side arms or carrying assault rifles, trying to look tough and mean. Whatever their posturing, none of Rodrigo's people looked happy to see him. But this was his moment, and he wasn't going to be denied. It fleeted through his mind that none of them might leave the Rodrigo estate in North Miami Beach alive. But he was the man of the hour, and he was going to make the Colombians a deal they were in no position to turn down.

It was a huge estate, and Stiles found himself impressed by the sprawling compound, the place swathed in palm trees and flowers, all kind of jungle vegetation. The mansion was white, everything pillared and gleaming, with a fountain right in the middle of the circular drive. Nothing but Porsches, Jags and Caddies stood in the driveway—nothing but the best.

They were coming down the steps, and Stiles rode his motorcycle straight for the group gathering in the driveway. Engines were shut down, and the Devil's Horsemen dismounted their bikes or piled out of the two vans. Stiles picked up the satchel he hoped would be his olive branch.

Right away, the biker leader saw the gunmen make a move to disarm them. One of the soldiers reached for his Browning, but Stiles draped a hand over the weapon. He smiled at the big man in the silk jacket.

"I don't think so, *hombre*."

"Let them keep their weapons."

Stiles sought out the voice and saw a slight figure in a silk shirt and white slacks step away from the group of gunmen. The dark-skinned man had a po-nytail that fell halfway down his back, and had enough diamonds and gold dangling off him, it seemed, to feed a Third World country for a month.

Stiles was still smiling as the man walked straight up to them. "Are you Juan Carlos or Fernando?"

"I'm Juan," the younger brother answered. "You are either insane, stupid or very brave, amigo."

"I'll settle for just plain old smart."

Juan Carlos Rodrigo looked at the satchel. "What's that?"

"A peace offering, a proposition, my trump card. Pick one."

Rodrigo scowled when he spotted Carlos Miniguez. "I recognize that man. He works for the Arguello bunch."

"He did, Juan," Stiles said. "But he's got something I'm sure you'll want to hear. It's about a traitor in your ranks."

Juan Carlos Rodrigo peered at Stiles for a moment, measuring the biker. "Inside. Follow me."

Moments later, Stiles and his men, trailing Rodrigo and flanked by Colombian gunmen, found himself even more impressed by the inside of the mansion. Everything was white, made of stone or coral or marble, Stiles guessed. More palm trees and flowers, even parrots and other exotic birds in small cages, decorated the sprawling living room. An entire area, sunken in the middle of the living room, was lined with a plush white couch, coffee table, giant screen TV and a small bar. The ceiling rafters were white, Stiles observed, maybe marble, wrapped in vines and other jungle vegetation. Stiles whistled.

"You guys have done pretty good for yourselves," the biker leader commented. "Sure looks to this gringo stud like it's time you shared some of the wealth with some homegrown red-blooded Americans."

Rodrigo glared at Stiles but said nothing.

Finally, Stiles and his crew were led into what he believed was some sort of conference room. The other brother was sitting, alone, at the end of a long white marble table. At first glance, Stiles decided Fernando Rodrigo wasn't much to look at, small and wiry, but there was something cold and deadly in the man's dark eyes. The Colombian was scowling as the bikers entered the room, and Stiles detected the glint of murderous insanity in his gaze.

Stiles tossed the satchel on the table. Fernando Rodrigo nodded at one of his men, who opened the satchel and displayed the bricks to his boss.

"There's only twenty bricks there," Stiles said. "I'm sitting on the rest."

The older brother ran a finger over his mustache. "What do you want?"

Stiles chuckled. "It's real simple. I want in. I want to be a part of your plans."

"That's absurd," Juan Carlos Rodrigo growled, moving behind Stiles, running a fierce gaze over the bikers. "You march in here, after ripping us off, and now you want to be one of us."

"You're playing a very dangerous game," Fernando said. "I could just kill you right now."

"Sure, you could. Then you'll never get the rest of your dope."

"Maybe we don't need it, maybe we can afford the loss," Fernando said.

"Maybe. Or maybe I can make your life a living hell." Stiles held his ground. "Or maybe we can do business. You seem to forget something here." He jerked a nod at Miniguez. "That man knows of a traitor, right under your nose. It's how we were able to stop you from getting ripped off. Hell, we saved the day for you people. I figure we're owed."

Fernando Rodrigo chuckled. "You're owed?"

"You're goddamn right."

"Do you know who you're fucking with?" the younger brother snarled.

"You bet I do. A couple of fucking grease monkeys who are flooding this country with cocaine and heroin, who got more money than they know what to do with it—who'll go down, not by the cops, but the Devil's Horsemen, hard and final. I'll take every last one of you out, if you force me to. I always get what I want."

Angry silence lingered for a full half-minute as the brothers stared at each other. Any second, Stiles was braced to draw his Browning and blast his way out of there.

Finally, Fernando Rodrigo looked at Miniguez. "Who?"

Before the Cali snitch could answer, Stiles barked, "Keep your mouth shut."

Then he turned to the brothers. "Not so fast. Look, I'm willing to trade here. I've come to work with you, not against you."

"What is it you propose to fix this situation?" Fernando Rodrigo asked.

"Simple. Bring us into the network. We've got contacts and connections in several states. Bike gangs that can help you move your stuff."

Fernando Rodrigo's gaze narrowed. "I'm listening."

"Second, we can enforce for you, maybe spearhead a run, since I'm pretty sure you move big loads out of state by semi trucks. The heat comes down, say, the law pulls one of your truckers over, we're there to take care of business."

Fernando Rodrigo grunted. "That's it? That's all you want?"

"Not quite. I get to keep one hundred keys. Let's call it a recovery fee. And a show of good faith on your part."

"You ask a lot," Fernando Rodrigo said. "You know so much, I assume you must know who my current partner is?"

"Yeah, the Tartaglia Family. So go talk to them and convince them it's in everyone's best interest to play ball with us."

The brothers both stared at Stiles, then looked at each other.

Fernando Rodrigo spoke. "I want my drugs back."

"And I want an answer."

"It's not that simple," the older brother said. "This is something I need to discuss with my would-be partners. It's something I have to think about."

"You've got until tomorrow. I'll be staying close. When I come back here, no, better yet, I'll call you by noon tomorrow, you better not disappoint me."

Juan Carlos Rodrigo nodded at Miniguez. "And that one?"

Stiles grinned at Miniguez, who suddenly wore a look of terror. "He's all yours. That will be my show of good faith."

Miniguez looked set to pounce on Stiles. He took a step toward the bike leader, his teeth bared. "You bastard!"

Two gunmen grabbed Miniguez.

"Hey, they don't call me Judas for nothing."

Smiling, Stiles put one last look on the Rodrigo

brothers then led his Devil's Horsemen out of the room.

WHEN THEY WERE CLEAR of Parker's estate and Grimaldi was driving west across Miami, Bolan used the cellular phone to call Special Agent Tasker. Two rings and Tasker's voice came through.

"It's Belasko. You've got a situation you need to know about."

"I got a situation? It looks like you and Griswald have been real busy upsetting the Don again. You know, there are people over here who can see that firestorm you touched off clear across town. What did you use? An A-bomb? How the hell did you pull that off?"

"We had a little luck. Listen to me real carefully. I've got it from a reliable source Tartaglia's got a couple of guys on the inside of either your task force, or the DEA, who are keeping him up to speed on what we're doing."

There was a pause on the other end. Bolan could only imagine how hard the man was taking the revelation.

"What source?" Tasker growled.

"Never mind that. You need to get Fromer to another location. You might start looking at your own people, the ones you might feel a little dubious about. Maybe a guy with money problems, or a new member of the team."

"You're crazy, Belasko. All my men are aboveboard."

"If you want to risk a hit, that's your business,

but consider yourself warned. Why do you make it sound like it's so impossible? Why do you think all these years Tartaglia's been one step ahead of you? It isn't because he's that smart. He's got people on our side in his pocket.''

"All right, all right. I'm going to work on the assumption you're onto something. I'll do it. But, hey, Belasko, what makes you think I might not be the guy in Tartaglia's pocket?''

"Wishful thinking.''

"Thanks for the vote of confidence.''

"I'll stay in touch. First, I need you to give me the address of one or both of the Rodrigo brothers' homes.''

Tasker heaved a sigh. "They live in the same place.'' The special agent gave Bolan the address. "Listen, don't screw this up. I've been informed by my own sources the deal is going down tomorrow. You hit Rodrigo, start wasting his people, we'll never dismantle his organization. For all I know, they're ready to pull up stakes in Miami and disappear to their homeland. If that happens, well, let's just say Colombian authorities have proved themselves a little uncooperative with us gringos.''

"Hang tough. I've got a plan. Just let me stick to it. Hey, you gave me forty-eight hours, right?''

"You're on the clock, Belasko, and I don't think I can hold off the city's finest much longer. Page me,'' Tasker added, and gave Bolan his pager number. "I guess I'll just have to watch the news to stay posted on your next move.''

"I'll get back to you," Bolan said and ended the connection.

The lights of Miami became distant beacons to Bolan as he sat in hard silence. He had given Grimaldi the directions and the address of the bar where Waters frequented, thanks to Parker.

"Another mess we left behind, Sarge. I wonder how the Don will handle this one. Not to mention if Parker's right about the sellout in the DEA, Tartaglia will have our descriptions. He'll field an army to nail us."

"I'm changing our game plan, Jack."

Grimaldi gave his friend a sideways look. "How so?"

"This is our last stop for the night. I'm going to have a little talk with the man who moves the Don's poison out of the state."

"If he's in a bar, it's a public place."

"No rough stuff, if I can avoid it. I'll have a heart-to-heart with the man over a beer."

"Make him see the light."

"Something like that."

"What next?"

"We go back to the base in the Everglades. I'll pick up the war wagon. I want you on standby, ready to fly the second I call you. If I'm right, if what we're hearing is taking us in the right direction, the stuff is coming in. If it slips past me, it'll be going up I-95 by tractor trailer."

Grimaldi's smile was grim. "How come I get the

feeling before this is over we're going to be involved in some air-and-ground tag team?''

"From here on, Jack, the winner is the last survivor.''

9

They found the bar at the edge of a large shopping center on the west side of town.

Bolan gave the lot a thorough scouring. Even at that early-morning hour, when most people were at home, asleep in bed, the soldier spotted enough vans, older model cars and pickup trucks strung around the bar to tell him they were partying the night away.

According to Parker, it was a joint that stayed open well into the night, accommodating truckers and other workers who were supposed to be on twenty-four-hour alert to load and move the Don's narcotics at Tartaglia's whim. What Bolan would be walking into, he could only guess. And how he'd play it out he'd leave up to Waters or whoever else might enter the picture.

No matter what, the soldier was braced for the worst-case scenario.

Grimaldi angled the sedan deep across the lot, away from the lampposts, finally parking the vehicle in the darkness between some palm trees. Across the lot, Bolan saw the apartment complexes, the sleepy suburbs. They had already made a drive-by of the large trucking company the Don owned north of the lot. It had looked like a massive place, maybe a half-dozen warehouses, each one as large as the drug lab they had blown up. Once again, Tartaglia kept that place of business close to the Expressway.

"Keep your eyes peeled, Jack," Bolan said, opening the door, zipping his windbreaker. The .44 Magnum Desert Eagle pistol rode on his hip, while the Beretta was in its shoulder holster.

"Give it fifteen minutes? Or if I hear all hell breaking loose inside?"

Bolan showed his friend a grim smile. "I'm hoping to work this one on the quiet side."

Grimaldi returned the smile. "In that case, I'm going to wish you luck."

Bolan moved across the lot, alert for any movement that looked out of the ordinary. He knew the two of them were already marked men.

Everything was on the line for Tartaglia. The Don's entire world was ready to go straight down the toilet, and the Executioner knew the man would spare no one and nothing to burn down the ones who had made his life miserable. Too many times, the Executioner had faced the savages of organized crime, and was all too grimly and painfully familiar with their ways. When their world was threatened, the cannibals always turned it up a notch—meaning everyone became fair game. And with all the drugs Tartaglia was looking to save, it would get uglier from there on.

Bolan knew that major narcotics traffickers often factored in losing a load here and there, as the cost of doing business. For every major load that was seized entering the country, another ten slipped through. From what he'd seen here so far, Bolan knew that narcotics was still the biggest game for organized crime in town, in the whole country, in fact.

And the big loads were stored just like Bolan and Grimaldi had found in the industrial park. That had been a major victory in the campaign, but it was far from over, Bolan knew. No doubt the Don would seethe the night away when word reached him of his latest embrace of disaster. Complications were going to arise, and the soldier had to be ready for anything to go wrong at anytime. It was one thing to take ten keys and bust up his swank strip joint, but when a major player had two or three tons go up in flames, it was something that would call for nothing short of all-out war.

Moments later, Bolan was inside the bar. The laughter was low, the country music from the juke-box solemn but loud enough to mute normal conversation. Several groups of burly men were shooting pool in the far corner of the place, lounging and drinking around three tables. There were enough pinball machines and dartboards in the game room to keep everyone occupied or amused, but Bolan figured the naked blond woman doing some table topping was the main attraction here.

The soldier caught a few suspicious looks, the usual sullen hostility a stranger would receive. Bolan gave the place a roving search. At the bar, he waited a few unnecessary moments before the bartender saw fit to make his way toward him. It gave Bolan time to pick out Mike Waters.

Parker's description of the man was perfect—big, balding guy in his early forties, with massive shoulders and a handlebar mustache, and a tattoo of a cobra on a bowling ball-sized right bicep. Bolan had his man.

A part of Bolan had expected to find a working stiff version of one of Tartaglia's button men, grim-faced and mean-eyed, ready to kill or maim in an eyeblink. Instead, Bolan sensed something else about Waters. For one thing, the trucker was drinking alone. While everyone else there was putting on the pretense of having a good old time, mixing it up with a few of the women, Waters appeared to Bolan like a man who was an hour away from walking to the electric chair. Indeed, there was something in the man's eyes that told the soldier that Waters was looking for an out, for some flicker of hope in a world that had become vicious, greedy and ugly beyond his comprehension. The guy was reachable. Maybe. It was just a hunch, but Bolan was going to play it.

"You want something, buddy?" the bartender gruffed.

"Whatever's on tap."

Bolan waited until the potbellied, scowling bartender came back, putting his glass down a little too hard on the counter. He paid the man, then made his way toward Waters. Closing on the table, Waters looked up at Bolan. Up close now, the soldier was sure the guy was running scared and wanted out.

Still, the trucker had to keep up appearances, so he put a little edge in his voice as he said, "Yeah?"

"Mike Waters?"

"Who's asking?"

"The ghost of all your troubles past."

Waters peered at the ice in Bolan's eyes, then ran a gaze over the soldier's jacket. "You're him, aren't you? The one I heard is kicking the man's ass all over this city."

"I want to talk."

"About what?"

"Your future. As in whether you'll have one."

Waters gave his surroundings a quick paranoid search. No one seemed to be paying attention to either of them.

"Why don't you have a seat, friend? If you are who I think you are, I couldn't very well stop you, could I?"

Bolan sat, his back to the wall, able to watch the door and everyone in the place. On the surface, all looked normal, but the soldier hadn't survived this long by taking anything for granted.

"I'm looking at you, Waters, and I see a man who doesn't like where he's been or what he's doing. If I'm wrong, feel free to correct me, but I don't think so."

Waters took a deep sip of his drink, then fired up a cigarette. "How many people you know, pal, who like their jobs, anyway?"

"I'm going to lay it out for you. It's going to be your call. Here it is, and if you think you know what I've been doing today, then you know this is a one-time offer. Your boss is going down, and when I say that, it means he won't be seeing a long stretch in prison. He's dealing with some new players in town, involving a megashipment of poison, I believe, which is either en route, or already here, and his new partners are going out the same way. I want you to think about it, real hard. The ones in this who are borderline have been offered a second chance.''

Waters grunted. He called a waitress over, ordered a shot of whiskey and two beers. Bolan sipped his own beer, waiting for Waters to speak. Something was working in the man's eyes, a change, some spark of hope perhaps. Either way, Bolan saw the man wrestling with his own demons.

The waitress came back with the drinks, and the trucker told her to put it on his tab.

''I've been doing this for ten years for him,'' Waters began when the waitress left. ''Ten years I've been taking ten grand a month in cash. I hang here or at the office, around-the-clock, waiting on the guy's men to give me the word, or get the word from him personally. I round up the crews, take the trucks, wherever, load up and get it moving out of state. I guess you and me, we don't need to put a name on what I'm talking about. You know the score. Hell, I don't know how long you been down here, aside from today obviously, or how much you've seen of this town. But this is the city that snow built. This shopping center alone just sprang up in the last year. I understand it was somewhere in the billion-dollar range. It's just a drop in the bucket, pal. You got more shopping centers, more malls, more condos and new hotels going up all over town, clear to Orlando even. There's more real-estate development in Florida than twenty states put together. And it all comes from dirty money. I mean it may come through the network, cleaned up, sugarcoated, through their realtors and bankers, but it's all the same. Dirty.'' Waters killed his shot.

"Yeah, okay, you read me right, mister, whoever you are. I know men, and I don't like the look of you. You're way beyond trouble, friend. You're here, all right, to make sure the king is dead.'' Waters stared hard at Bolan. "Yeah, I want out. I've been wanting out for a long, long time, but I don't know how to do it. I've got a wife and three kids. I mean I got a solid marriage and a beautiful family. She doesn't have a clue. She never asks where the money comes from. She just figures I'm putting in all these long hours, and it's paying off in a sweet bonus. She doesn't even know who it is I really work for.

"We take a couple trips down to the Caribbean every year, the kids go to private school, we got nice cars, a nice home up in Hialeah. But I'm just as dirty as he is, maybe worse. At least he doesn't lie to himself about what he is, which is a predator, a destroyer of life. Me, I'm just a regular guy, but lying to myself and to my wife.... Yeah, you might say, friend, all of a sudden I'm getting a conscience. Or maybe I'm just plain scared.''

Bolan clenched his jaw. He wasn't about to cut Waters any slack for family values, but he sensed the man wanted his own second chance. Sometimes in life, Bolan knew, there were those who did wrong and wanted a second chance if they didn't cross a certain line from which there was no return. The Executioner was a believer in new life, in second chances. Provided, of course, the individual's heart was sincere. The soldier found himself wanting to believe in Waters. And from what he had seen so far, there were still people, even the borderline ones, worth fighting for, worthy of a chance to turn it around. Without hope, life became mean, and meaningless.

"It's already happening," Waters told Bolan. "I got one semi already loaded with a ton-and-a-half, Big Apple bound. But I've been told to hold off. It's this thing he's got with these new players you mentioned. I see guys like the Rodrigos down here all the time. They come and they go, but when one drops, five more spring up, like weeds, or cockroaches to take their place. These Cali brothers, I hear, are crazy. They're stone-cold killers, just like the guy I work for. And I'll tell you, just thinking about what I've been told to pick up, I mean the sheer size of this load, it's mind-boggling. I don't need to see the stuff. All I've got to do is look at the paperwork, how much citrus is really being loaded in a semi, as opposed to open space up front. I've been told to have four semis, ready to roll anytime. My question to you is, what are you offering me?"

"A second chance. A way to make it right."

Waters nodded, then killed one beer. "Okay. That's all I needed to hear."

The trucker started working on his second beer as Bolan told him to memorize two numbers. One was to contact Special Agent Tasker by beeper. The other number would be for the cellular phone Bolan would have once he rounded up the war wagon.

"Tell me some more about this deal," Bolan said. "You know when and where?"

"Not exactly when, but I've gotten the word from a source of where, and the boss called me here, about thirty minutes and four drinks ago, and confirmed it. It's a warehouse hangar the Rodrigos got. I can give you directions. I'm going to tell you this. The boss is sending a crew with this run, his own goons. He sometimes does that, but this time is something different, something I hear in Don Paolo's voice. Fear. I won't be going, I never do. I just make the shipping arrangements from the company. What it all tells me, is the boss is ready to go down in flames if those trucks are pulled over and searched. He's been on top for twenty years in this town, and I guess he figures his number is up. It happens to guys like that. They know they can't hold it forever." Waters paused to hit his beer. "What is it exactly you plan to do, if you don't mind me asking?"

"Something that not all the surveillance, stake-outs, wiretaps and front-door DEA raids can do."

Waters's smile was weary. "How come I figured that much out myself?"

GRIMALDI WAS WATCHING the lot, but he didn't see the two dark vehicles race out of the alley beside the bar until the last possible moment. By then, it was too late.

Maybe it was the light from the lampposts or the beams from their headlights washing over his vehicle, a fluke of the moment, a sudden bad twist of fate. Whatever, Grimaldi knew a crew of hardmen when he saw one. And each vehicle, he figured, held at least three guys, maybe four. One look at him, and he realized they knew who he was.

The pilot was reaching over the seat, hauling up the M-16 when the vehicles barreled toward him, cutting off any possible escape. Rubber was screeching and he glimpsed shadows disembarking, maybe twenty yards away. Before he knew it, submachine guns, large-caliber revolvers and pump shotguns were blazing away, blasting the windshield in a hurricane of glass. Ducking a millisecond before he was decapitated, Grimaldi burst out the door. Undoubtedly Bolan would hear the racket of weapons' fire and emerge from the bar, doing his best to seize back the night.

As autofire pounded the vehicle, Grimaldi hoped his friend wouldn't be too late. Just like that, the ace pilot found himself outgunned, outmanned, and, as he peered around the front end of the sedan, outmaneuvered.

At least eight hardmen were surging ahead, firing on the run.

Grimaldi was pinned down, with nowhere to go.

BOLAN WAS MOVING for the front door when he heard the sudden gunfire outside. Grimaldi was in serious trouble.

Drawing both the Desert Eagle and the Beretta, Bolan hit the door, pushing through with his shoulder like a human bulldozer. Surging across the sidewalk, he took in the battle site.

It didn't look good.

There were eight of them, all heavily armed. Two cars had apparently flown up on the sedan, and the enemy had bailed, moving hard and fast, to reach Grimaldi and end it quick.

Bolan got busy. It was a definite plus they had their backs to him, unaware of the lethal intent racing up on their blind side.

The Executioner changed that in the next moment. The .44 Magnum Desert Eagle boomed in his left hand, while the Beretta spit out a triburst of 9 mm rounds that zipped across the backs of three hardmen. The Desert Eagle roared again, the .44 hollowpoint projectile ripping through a gunner's lower back, launching him over the hood of a brandnew white Cadillac, blood washing the luxury vehicle in a fresh paint job.

The soldier figured there were four down, but the rest were pumped and whirling, tracking him with their variety of hardware. In the heat of battle, Bolan couldn't be sure how many were dropped, and how many were left. Only one way to find out.

Triggering his weapons on the fly, Bolan vaulted over the hood of a parked vehicle. He scored another hit and saw the guy clutch his upper chest, go down, screaming in agony.

Pump actions were jacked on two enemy shotguns. Thunder roared over the lot and Bolan was forced to the ground as buckshot and bullets exploded every piece of glass on the vehicle marking his cover. The soldier darted for another parked car, but glimpsed a figure by the sedan pop up and cut loose with an M-16.

At least, Bolan knew Grimaldi was alive.

And kicking. The ace pilot marched a leaden storm of 5.56 mm slugs through the next hardman. Then, a quick blast from Grimaldi's Ithaca pump shotgun and the gunman was kicked to the asphalt.

Bolan moved for the cover of another vehicle, outflanking the enemy. Now the hardmen were pinched in. They had been so consumed with charging Grimaldi that they had neglected to think a gunman could suddenly come roaring at them from the bar.

It proved their one big and very fatal mistake.

They tried to seek cover by their vehicles, but Grimaldi poured on the blistering autofire.

Bolan walked ahead, both weapons thundering, hammering out more slugs. The three remaining gunners never made their vehicles, nor did they ever know what hit them. One by one they cried out as bullets tore into them and flung them all over the lot.

Then one wounded gunman staggered to his feet, his chest soaked in crimson. He started to lift an Uzi submachine gun toward Bolan, snarling, "You're the goddamn bastard's been hitting us, ain't ya?"

One mighty thunderclap from the Executioner's Desert Eagle put the guy's question to eternal rest.

Bolan saw people rushing out of the bar, but he was already racing for the sedan. As luck would have it, no bullets had punctured the tires or drilled through the engine. Grimaldi was gunning the engine to life as Bolan dropped through the door.

Flooring the gas pedal, Grimaldi patched rubber out of there. Bolan didn't look back, hoping they got clear and free of Miami before the cops threw down a net.

Either way, it was time to lay low for a while. Let Tartaglia lick his wounds.

The two soldiers needed to regroup, restrategize and assess what they had learned.

All the Executioner knew was that there was some serious heat in Miami right then. The next day it would get even hotter.

The kind of heat, Bolan thought, that would kill in droves.

10

Crisis was nothing new to either of the Rodrigo brothers. Many times in their lives they had confronted adversaries, traitors, informants, good cops and bad cops—the whole spectrum of players, solid and shaky, loyal and disloyal, all who inhabited the world they lived in. They always survived, simply because they dispatched their enemies with swift and brutal retribution. In fact, they'd take out a man's entire family, by machine gun or machete, it didn't matter. Torture and violent death always left a lingering message of fear to others that the brothers were a force to be reckoned with.

Only this time, too much was coming at them from too many sides, with sudden twists, mounting problems and human minefields hitting them all at once. Fernando Rodrigo wasn't worried about handling any situation, either with the Mafia, the bikers or the DEA for that matter, but he could tell his younger brother was clearly agitated and concerned. Crisis was solved by using brute force, plain and simple. To live in fear wasn't his way, Fernando Rodrigo thought. Power was seized and then only kept by putting fear into the hearts of others. And they were men of considerable power. This day would be the day where the Rodrigo brothers let everyone who was a major player in Miami know they had arrived, and were there to stay.

They were the new cartel.

Sipping his brandy, pacing around the massive coffee table in the sunken area of the living room, Fernando Rodrigo decided it was time to get his house in order. He fired up a cigarette and glanced at his brother, who was drinking tequila. The older man checked his diamond-studded Rolex watch. Tartaglia and his people would be arriving soon. He watched as his men, all of them armed with assault rifles or submachine guns, made the place ready for the arrival of their new partner. Most of their work was confined to a large table where money-counting machines were being set up, or they were simply standing guard over the two bloody pieces of quivering meat that once resembled something human.

Fernando Rodrigo looked at the pulped faces of both Carlos Miniguez and Ramon Suaro. The traitors were sprawled, groaning and rolling some in their blood, the plastic that had been spread out beneath them crinkling with their squirming weight. One of the soldiers kicked Suaro in the stomach as he tried to rise to his knees. The soldier called the man a dog, among other things, and ordered him to remain facedown in his blood.

Juan Carlos Rodrigo poured another tequila from the bar built into the low wall near the short steps that led up to the living room.

Again the older man read the concern on his

brother's face. He showed him an easy smile. "Relax, Juan, everything will be fine. Is it the DEA you're worried about?"

"No. With all these guns here, they wouldn't be crazy enough to raid us at this time. I'm glad, however, that our families are in Cali."

"Your family. I have only a woman, and two children by other women. You are married with four young children by the same beautiful lady. But, I understand, there are no women or children around now to worry about in case, as the Americans say, it hits the fan." He laughed. "I love times like this, my brother. A man, my brother, wins at all costs. He triumphs in the face of adversity. He proves to the world what it is to be a man. This is no time to fret like a woman over the problems we face."

"You're going to do business with the biker trash?"

"Ah, that is what you're worried about. I don't see any other way."

"It's dangerous. They're wild animals."

"I want our drugs back. When the wild animal calls, I'll tell him he is in on this run."

"That is insane. You can't! Tartaglia will never agree to that."

"I'll go ahead and do it before I tell him. I can make the man see reason. What can it hurt? Have the biker trash trail the man's tractor trailers at a safe distance and make them feel like they are a part of things. It's too late. We have already made the arrangements for the Don of Miami to pick up his shipment today. He's anxious to move the product out of the state. If we don't deal with the bikers, they'll cause us more problems than if we let them in. I see no other way, my brother. At least not now. Later, we can decide what to do with them. Maybe they'll prove themselves valuable.''

Juan Carlos Rodrigo shook his head. "It's risky, too dangerous to deal with these bikers. They could ruin everything for us.''

The older Colombian watched his brother kill the tequila. ''Since when have we ever worried about risk? We, who were street orphans in Cali. We, who were thieves that stole just to survive and later became assassins and couriers for the men who used to be in power in our country. We, who demanded and carved out our own turf. We are two of the most powerful men of what others call the Cali Cartel, only we're the new blood, with the promise of being bigger than any of them ever even dreamed possible. We have dozens of jungle labs, many of them underground, and the safest and most legitimate shipping routes in the world. We have more product ready to move than we know what to do with, much of it already here in this country. We have legitimate businesses, real-estate investors who are handling so much of our money, we can create a boom of hotels, condominiums, restaurants and shopping centers. We could quite literally own this city in two years. It's all we have worked and hoped for. Now, last night was a mistake, I'll grant that. No more midnight runs over the swamp. No more mistakes.''

''That's another problem you touched on. We've become too big, too fast.''

"Which is why I feel we must return to Cali in the next day or so. For maybe a month or two. There's business down there we must stabilize, new deals to make." He looked at the bloody forms on the floor. "There are two problems we have already taken care of. Ramon, who I trusted with every detail of our operations, sells out to our rivals, small and jealous men, and for money. The other one comes sniveling to us, saying he's no longer happy with his Family. Who can you trust? Not a dog certainly who is loyal to no master. Loose tongues and treachery must be laid to rest. It's how they all go down. Someone gets greedy or becomes unhappy and talks to the authorities. Men in our position can't afford to get careless, nor can we show mercy to traitors. We can't, we won't fall, or we'll die before we lose all we have worked so hard and risked so much to attain. Today will be just one crowning achievement in a future of glory and more riches than any man in our business has ever known. Especially now that we're bringing a new product into this country."

His brother nodded, even smiled. Heroin. The future was, indeed, theirs for the taking. Even as they spoke, new markets for heroin were being opened up by their distributors, poppy being grown and harvested across the Andes by countless acres. They were huge, they both knew it, and they were getting bigger every day.

Suddenly, the voice of Suaro cracked through the living room. "Fernando, please, I beg you, I was merely frightened of a war coming down on us."

"Silence!" the younger brother erupted, hurling his glass, which struck Sauro in the face. "Our men found you packing your bags, with a plane ticket for Cali and a suitcase with close to a million dollars U.S. What were you going to do? Go to the authorities in Colombia and make sure we spent the rest of our lives in their prison? Or hiding in the jungle?"

Rodrigo nodded at one of his soldiers. "Do it."

"Something we must consider and discuss now. What of this problem Tartaglia is having?" the younger drug lord said. "All of a sudden he's at war, or rather someone has declared war on him and on the eve of both our sides finalizing our deal."

The older man poured another brandy as two soldiers brought a ladder into the living room. It was troubling, but again, it was something they'd deal with. "What of it? We hear it's two gringos who are seeking to destroy the man, for whatever reason. Wild dogs. Certainly not any DEA or any other law-enforcement agency would be running on the loose around this city, killing his people, destroying his places of business."

"His problems could become our problems, Fernando."

Rodrigo smiled as the ladder was rested against the ceiling rafter. Two thick ropes were secured to the beam and dropped to the living-room floor where nooses were quickly made by his soldiers. A small portable hydraulic lift had been wheeled in and set up in the middle of the room. Fernando Rodrigo saw his men had shortened the rope just enough to hang his personal message of retribution at least ten feet off the floor.

"That's just it, my brother. We're all in this together. Too much is at stake. One of us falls, all of us falls. Tartaglia knows that."

"You are the older brother, Fernando. I've always worshiped you, trusted your judgment." He shrugged, "It'll be no different this time."

The brothers embraced. It was good to have solidarity in a time of crisis, Fernando Rodrigo thought. The younger man made the both of them another drink.

Suddenly there was a commotion up top. The brothers watched as gags were stuffed into the mouths of the traitors, the nooses slipped over their heads, tightened around their necks. Muffled cries of terror sounded through the living room. It was a chore for his soldiers, but they finally beat and pummeled the two traitors onto the lift.

Puffing on his cigarette, Fernando Rodrigo looked at one of his soldiers, smiled, and said, "Sanchez, what's for breakfast?"

THE NIGHT HAD PASSED in anxious preparations for the coming day, with Bolan and Grimaldi catching maybe two hours of restless sleep at the base.

This was the day the two soldiers launched all-out war against the Tartaglia-Rodrigo connection. It was the beginning of the ultimate end for the two biggest narcotics traffickers in South Florida.

Bolan walked out of the large tent to find Grimaldi checking over the gunship in a clearing near the edge of some cypress trees. Their base was deep in a wooded area, roughly forty miles southwest of Miami, near the West Dade Expressway. Dawn had broken over the forest, shadows removed from the earth, as if seared away by the rising sun that burned from a cloudless sky.

The supreme efficiency Brognola always displayed never failed to amaze Bolan. But he knew the big Fed expected nothing less than utter commitment from himself and his warriors, wanted nothing short of total success on a mission, even though he knew his Stony Man soldiers were always one bullet away from not returning from a campaign.

Man, machine and equipment on the makeshift Florida base had been trucked in or flown down from the Farm, including the large fuel bins for the gunship and Bolan's custom war wagon. Three blacksuits from Stony Man had stayed on base, around-the-clock, and would remain there until the mission was finished.

Bolan had spent most of the night with Grimaldi going over what they knew, how they were going to proceed. Brognola had cut the necessary red tape with the proper authorities to get Grimaldi his airspace. Bolan didn't need details; he always knew Brognola just got the job done.

Results were all that mattered.

Grimaldi was looking at his helicopter. The gunship had been built, piece by piece, at Stony Man by a team of aeroengineers. Bolan looked at the black copter, which resembled in shape and specs the Bell Huey that was the helicopter warbird of

Vietnam. Only this one was upgraded and updated with state-of-the-art radar, antiradar and tracking equipment, along with an auxiliary fuel tank to stretch its range. Rocket pods with 40 mm grenades were portside, and four TOW missiles with an M-60 machine gun in the doorway on the starboard side. Add a machine gun in the nose that fired armor-piercing rounds, with everything designed to be electronically unleashed by a gunstick. Best of all, it had been custom-built to be handled by one pilot. And Jack Grimaldi, Bolan knew, was the ace of top guns. Code-named Predator, it would most certainly rain death from above. Grimaldi patted the fuselage, looking anxious to get the gunship airborne.

"We're on-line?" the pilot asked. "The big Fed's up-to-speed and giving us the thumbs-up?"

Bolan informed Grimaldi everything was set. It was going to be touch-and-go once the load was pinpointed and they were locked on for a coordinated ground-and-air assault. Bolan knew Grimaldi was worried about any fighter jets that might get into the act, maybe Homestead Air Force Base going on full alert at some future point. The soldier assured Grimaldi that Brognola had cleared the way. Still, Murphy's Law could reach out and touch them anytime. Pros with much hard-earned battlefield experience, they knew and understood the grim reality of having to adjust to whatever situation arose. It certainly helped they both knew that, if necessary, the Justice Man's clout reached all the way to the White House. There was a frequency on Grimaldi's radio that could patch through to Brognola if the situation in the air turned sticky.

It brought to mind Bolan's call to Special Agent Tasker a few hours before. Fromer had been moved to another safehouse, Tasker giving Bolan the address where the DEA team was situated in a Miami suburb. But Tasker was demanding to be in, now that the hour of doom seemed to be upon Tartaglia and the Rodrigos. Bolan had demanded a little more time. If the DEA raided the Rodrigo estate or tracked where the load was being delivered, the soldier had explained, a lot of Tasker's people were going to die. At this point, Bolan had seen and heard enough to know the narcotraffickers were forging ahead with a business as usual approach, maybe even determined to the point of a suicidal fury to save their kingdom. Tasker backed off, but said he'd be monitoring the situation. Bolan didn't press it, but he hoped the DEA stayed in the background. As for Waters, Bolan would call the man later, once he got his own surveillance underway. Of course, given what had happened in the parking lot at the bar, everything could've changed. But Bolan was counting on the trucker holding himself together if grilled by Tartaglia.

Together, Bolan and Grimaldi walked to the war wagon. The pilot gave a whistle as he ran another appreciative gaze over the custom black van. Bolan had been thoroughly briefed, shown and even given the war wagon a test run at Stony Man before heading out for the Miami campaign.

It was a formidable piece of equipment. Portside

and starboard, the doors could open from the touch of one of three electronic gunsticks, and one M-60 machine gun on a swivel mount on either side could extend from the van. Aft, a 20 mm cannon could pound out its devastation, again firing from between doors that were electronically opened. But there was even more firepower. The floorboard could be opened by the control panel next to the radio console. A box would release a dozen Claymore mines. Once the mines were dropped, they were all locked into the same radio frequency on the control panel that Bolan could activate with a flick of a switch. It was all or nothing once those mines were dropped. Half of the mines were of C-4 composition, the other six ready to blow enough white phosphorous over a fifty-yard radius to incinerate anything that moved. The van's hull was armor plated, and the windshield and windows were bullet-resistant. Still, none of it might hold up completely under a steady onslaught of weapons' fire.

It was all touch-and-go, bolan thought. With what they knew and suspected they'd be facing, there was no other way than to use the hardware they had. If nothing else, they'd come prepared.

"Hal said to bring everything back in one piece," Grimaldi said.

"The man lives in hope."

"Don't we all."

"I'll call you once I learn something."

"Good luck, Sarge. Something tells me we're going to need a little extra help from the fickle hand of fate on this one."

Bolan nodded as he hopped into the van. Didn't he know it.

STILES PUT THE PHONE down, grinned at his men, then shot a thumbs-up.

"It's a go," he told them. "We're in. Our Colombian brothers have seen the light."

They were holed up in an apartment near the Robert Frost Expressway, a few blocks east of the Miami River. The place was rented by a friend of Peaches, and Stiles had made the apartment his temporary command post, barging in and getting the girlfriends of his old lady under control with a slap and a promise of some coke. It was close enough to the Rodrigo estate so that Stiles felt near the action. Apparently, the action was happening. Fast.

"I got directions to a place west of the Palmetto Expressway," he told his men. "We're to meet the brothers there at three o'clock. They said we'll get our assignments then."

"What if he's setting us up?" Brewer wanted to know.

Stiles understood their concern, but he liked what he saw on their faces. All of them were wild-eyed, had mean grins on their lips, were pumped on adrenaline. He had ridden with these men long enough to know that they all knew the score. There was no turning back, no stopping now. Victory or death. There was no other way. If someone even looked at them funny, they'd beat him to a bloody pulp. Cop, dealer, citizen, whatever. That was their way, the only way to get respect. Kick ass.

"We've got some time to kill. I need to call back to the compound anyway. Get the others to saddle up and be ready to ride."

TARTAGLIA WAS STUNNED the moment he entered the Rodrigo mansion. The first thing he saw, hell, couldn't help but notice, were the two bodies, hung by the neck, from the ceiling. Lifeless eyes seemed to seek out the Don from those contorted death masks. Surrounded by four of his soldiers, his counsel and his moneymen, Tartaglia stopped cold in his tracks at the edge of the hall. He was long since hardened to the sight of violent death, had been directly or indirectly involved in torture himself, but hanging people in your own home was something of a shock, even to his system. He could tell his lawyer, Parker, and his moneymen were also unnerved by the lynching. He knew he had a what-the-hell look on his face the second he stepped into the living room. He was greeted by big smiles on the faces of the Rodrigos, and it was the older one who was quick to explain the situation about the traitors he'd uncovered, right under his nose. He expressed his apologies. He could explain.

Once the formalities were out of the way and explanations made to calm nerves, drinks were built and passed out. Then the duffel bags were opened with stacks of hundreds quickly pulled out to then be run through the money-counting machines.

Eventually, they got down to business but Tartaglia felt anything but calm. The display he saw in the living room confirmed that the Rodrigos were as crazy as he had been warned they were, maybe a little too crazy to do business with. But Tartaglia needed that load now, more than ever, especially after all that had happened. In short, he was stuck and had to put on the best business face he could muster.

Scotch whiskey in hand, Tartaglia followed the brothers down into the sunken area where he settled into the couch.

The Don sipped his drink and looked at the dead men hanged behind him. "I'd say you two certainly got a flare for the dramatic."

"They deserved it, I assure you," the older brother said, grinning.

They made a toast, pledging to a long and prosperous relationship.

Then Tartaglia was told about the bikers. He felt his jaw drop in disbelief, barely hearing himself say, "What?"

He was told the brothers would handle the bikers, in fact, they apologized, but they had already made arrangements to give the bikers the go-ahead, or at least let the bikers think they were in for the long haul. A lot of product was missing, being sat on by these animals who called themselves the Devil's Horsemen. The brothers wanted their drugs back, at all cost. And who knew? Maybe the bikers might prove themselves a new source for distribution, but that was later down the road. After all, there was so much product they had on hand, they needed new distributors. They asked Don Paolo to kindly understand and grant them this one wish. Later they could work out the logistics of slipping the bikers in on the run.

All Tartaglia saw was another problem on top of all the ones he already had. He'd lost more soldiers the previous night. First, Parker had been hit, roughed up by two guys, which his lawyer had called "home invaders," but Tartaglia knew who they were—the hitters, causing him still more misery, more anxiety and paranoia. There were a lot of unanswered questions on Parker's part. And everyone around him was on edge.

Tartaglia didn't like it, none of it, but he told the Rodrigos to handle these bikers and not let them become his problem.

"We'll iron out some details," Fernando Rodrigo said. "Then we must go."

Tartaglia caught the gleam in the man's eyes, felt his eyebrow lift. "Are you trying to tell me what I think you are?"

"I told you to be ready to move right away," the older brother said. "Yes, your merchandise is already here."

It was the best news Tartaglia had heard since the previous day, but he had already suspected the product was nearby. And for the first time in what felt like an eternity, Don Paolo smiled.

BOLAN WAS DRIVING around the business district in north Miami. It was getting late in the morning, and he was wondering how to proceed. He decided he'd get close to the Rodrigo estate, park, then leg it in for a soft probe, if possible. He was dressed in black, and his webbing, Ka-bar, frag grenades and his Uzi subgun were behind him, near the 20 mm cannon.

He could feel time running out. He needed to touch base with Waters soon.

Bolan came to a light at an intersection, decided to turn left and head on a northeast route for the Rodrigo compound when he heard a sudden peal of rubber, coming up on the driver's side. Looking through his dark aviator shades, he turned and found a group of bikers sliding up, almost on top of his door. They were staring him down, scowling. As hot as he was, he knew he didn't need any displays of public trouble. And the Executioner read them as certain trouble, was sure of it when he spotted the bulges of side arms tucked in their waistbands, beneath their denim jackets. The insignia on the back of their jackets caught his eye. Devil's Horsemen. He could believe it.

He looked away, but then one of them cursed and wanted to know what the hell he was looking at. The guy barked the question again. Not good. He wanted to ignore them, but discovered in the next moment that was the worst course of action. For some reason a huge biker with a shaved head slid off his bike and came looming up in Bolan's side-view glass.

"Man asked you a question," the shaved head biker was snarling.

The Executioner didn't have time for this. The light was staying red a long time. If he made a run for it, he would draw attention from maybe a roving police cruiser, or maybe these guys were crazy enough to chase him all over town.

Just as the shaved head biker reached for his door handle, Bolan chose the only course of action possible.

The Executioner drew the .44 Magnum Desert Eagle, threw a shoulder into the door and thrust the mammoth hand cannon in the biker's face.

11

Bolan commanded their undivided attention. The bikers froze, but the Executioner sensed the standoff was on the verge of erupting and it could go to hell, right there on the street. And there were plenty of witnesses, also paralyzed, Bolan saw from the corner of his eye, who could identify him.

Ice in his eyes, Bolan stared up at the giant bald biker and said, "I suggest you get on your bike and ride on."

There was a flicker of defiance in the wild eyes of the shaved-head biker that warned Bolan he might make a sudden and very stupid play, even if it meant getting his head blown off in broad daylight. Bolan put some pressure on the Desert Eagle, jamming the muzzle a little deeper in the soft flesh under the biker's jaw.

"Pull that piece away from my face, and me and you go at it, right now, right here," the biker snarled, his eyes bulging with demonic fury.

"Brewer, forget him, man. Get on your horse and let's ride."

"I want his ass, Judas!"

"Get on your horse!"

Brewer didn't budge. Bolan caught the stench of liquor on the biker's breath. Worse, looking into the pinholes of his black eyes, the soldier knew the biker was jacked up on dope. Another second passed, the biker baring his teeth, then he backed off, sidling for his Harley, his burning stare locked on Bolan. Carefully the soldier watched them. Four of them were on bikes, and there was a black van just behind the Devil's Horsemen. Behind the windshield, bearded faces with angry eyes stared at Bolan. The Executioner caught a glimpse of the muzzle of an assault rifle from inside the van.

Holding his ground, Bolan looked at the biker with the shoulder-length black hair, the one who had ordered his man back on his bike. For a moment, the soldier was puzzled, but his combat senses stayed on full alert. One of their own had started trouble with a citizen, but a citizen with a very big gun. Bolan figured they should've finished what they started, just to save face. Something didn't feel right. The Devil's Horsemen were backing off too easily. Why? Something was happening with the bikers, all right, something they wanted to hide. The person Bolan assumed was their leader had shown what appeared unusual restraint, and there was a reason for it.

Moments later, they thundered through the intersection, then rounded the corner. Bolan waited until they were gone, before hopping inside his van. He surveyed the street. No cruisers were in the immediate area, and the sidewalk throngs seemed content to mind their own business. A damn close encounter of the worst kind was behind him. He'd gotten lucky, he hoped.

Bolan headed east. A moment's relief washing over him, he then began sorting out his next move. He declined a probe of the Rodrigo estate. It was best to go straight to the address of the suspected stash site Waters had given him and stake it out. The day was going to pass in tense waiting, it seemed, and Bolan was pumped to launch the final blow against the Tartaglia Family and the Rodrigos. Biding his time, waiting it out while the enemy made their next move wasn't his way. But it looked like he had no choice.

Unless he made something happen. More than likely, the soldier knew, he would have to do just that. Make it happen, burn all the enemy down but at a time and a place of his choosing. Of course, there was a good possibility it wouldn't fall that way. Bolan had become the hunted.

The Executioner wished Mike Waters would call and update him. Then the cellular phone rang. He picked it up, turned it on and said, "Yeah."

It was Waters. The man's timing was perfect. It was the big day for the megashipment, after all, and Waters clearly sounded nervous, on edge, maybe ready to bail. Clinging to hope for hard intel since his meet with Waters, Bolan had read the man as someone who would stay close in touch with the one person he believed could bail him out.

The man's voice sounded guarded, even as he tried to put on a good-old-boy front. Bolan listened, aware that the Don might have the phones on all of his key places of business tapped. Waters called Bolan "Johnny" and tried to keep it light. He told Bolan he was going to lunch in about an hour and gave the soldier the address of a small bar that was close to the trucking company, and he'd see him then. Bolan confirmed he'd be there, then hung up.

Some new development was underway. Good or downright grim, it sounded up for grabs. Whatever the Executioner thought he had detected in Waters's voice, he knew he could take nothing as it seemed. Had Tartaglia gotten to Waters? Would the man be followed by some of the Don's henchmen, ready to start blasting away on sight when they met up?

It's got to be played, Bolan told himself, taken as it showed. There was no other way.

Digging out his map of Miami to find the easiest route to his rendezvous with Waters, Bolan discovered another problem suddenly hitting his rear. He looked into the sideview mirror and spotted a dark blue four-door Ford with enough antennas to spot it as an unmarked unit from a quarter-mile away. The soldier was certain he was about to be picked up by Miami cops. He peered harder at the unmarked unit's reflection in the mirror, and Bolan recognized the familiar scowl of Agent Brockton, then he saw Tasker behind the wheel. Tasker started flashing his headlights.

Bolan found an alley and pulled in. With Tasker swinging in on his rear, Bolan rolled midway down the alley, stopped, then got out.

Tasker and Brockton emerged from their Ford. They slammed their doors with enough force to let

Bolan know this wasn't going to be a pleasant exchange. Both agents were now scowling from behind their dark sunglasses.

"No, Belasko," Tasker said, walking toward him, "we weren't following you. We spotted you about a block north of where you just had your little run-in with those bikers. That would've been real nice if you'd have blown that biker's head off. Oh, well, just another mess I've got to cover up for you."

Bolan saw Brockton giving his big custom van a hard eyeballing. There were no windows on the back doors, and Bolan only hoped Brockton didn't give the vehicle any further inspection. The Executioner stood, nearly hugging the driver's door, hoping it would be enough to keep Tasker or Brockton from moving toward the front where they could peer through the windshield. Bolan didn't have either the time or desire to explain the hardware inside. It would certainly speak for itself, and it would look to the agents exactly what it was. Bolan was outfitted to begin a street war.

Brockton's smile was sarcastic. "Van's more than a bit oversized, Belasko. What, you moving a couple grand pianos for the Don?"

Bolan ignored the man, then met Tasker's scowl. "I take it there's something you need to tell me?"

Tasker chuckled. "You bet there is. I can't hold off my operation any longer, and that's straight from my boss who said if your boss has a problem with that he'll deal with him. Just thought I'd let you know myself. We've got a tip that a container ship is stuffed with the biggest load of narcotics we've ever seized. It checks, all the way to our people in Colombia, and traces back to a Rodrigo-owned business in Cali.''

Bolan hid his surprise. Something didn't feel right to the soldier about this news. Tasker seemed a little too eager, too confident. It all looked too easy, too pat for the DEA. Bolan had his own theory. Such as the container ship was a decoy vessel. But he decided to keep it to himself and check it out with Waters.

"What have you checked, Tasker?" Bolan asked. "The documentation on the ship and its place of origin?"

Tasker balked, then peered at the soldier. "It's going to be boarded and raided this evening. It's about sixty miles southeast, as we speak, off Key West. The DEA, Coast Guard, every law-enforcement agency in South Florida is going to be on hand to tear that ship apart."

So Tasker knew beyond any doubt that a load of narcotics was on board.

"Are you inviting me to your victory celebration, gentlemen?" Bolan asked.

"What's your problem, Belasko?" Brockton growled. "Why do I get the feeling you act like you don't believe we'll find a damn thing on that boat except maybe a hull full of shrimp."

"It's the wrong move," Bolan said.

"Bullshit," Brockton shot back.

"Look, Belasko," Tasker intervened, taking a step toward him. "As of three o'clock tomorrow, the DEA has enough on Tartaglia and the Rodrigos to raid their homes and seize their businesses.''

Without any drugs, Bolan knew the bad guys would walk. He decided to let it ride, steer clear of any hint of antagonizing either agent. His hunch was the DEA was going to a lot of trouble for nothing. At this point, Bolan knew his way was the only solution to ridding the state of at least two major narcotraffickers.

"You know who those bikers were, Belasko, you pulled that cannon on?" Tasker said.

"I've a feeling you're going to tell me."

"We've had a team staked out near the Rodrigo estate. They rolled into their compound last night. Why, we're not sure. But there's some connection."

Brockton picked up the ball. "The Devil's Horsemen is an outlaw biker gang that used to deal crank. Maybe now they're looking to break in on some of the Cali turf, maybe deal for the Rodrigos. They'll be going down just like the rest of them."

It was certainly an angle that Bolan would look into. With or without this latest piece of news, the soldier knew he had a full plate.

"The whole Rodrigo compound," Tasker said, "looks to be on full alert. Nothing but their soldiers on the property. Not one of their women, not even a two-thousand-dollar-a-night call girl. Which means they're ready to go all the way, down with the ship."

Bolan mentally filed away everything Tasker told him. "You know where this bike gang is headquartered?"

Tasker shook his head. "You know something, Belasko, you ask for an awful lot. And so far you've given me nothing but grief. When this is over, I'm going to get hell as it is, keeping the Justice Department's involvement, your unconventional style of declaring war on the drug traffickers out of field reports, debriefs and definitely out of the media. In fact, I'm going to try and forget we ever met."

Bolan repeated his question, and Tasker told him where the Devil's Horsemen compound was located. Tasker said their headquarters had been under surveillance awhile back, but the investigation went nowhere. It was close enough, Bolan decided, to stop by and check them out himself.

"You find the leaks I warned you about?" the soldier asked.

Tasker and Brockton exchanged what Bolan thought was an embarrassed look.

"Two of our agents are missing," Tasker said. "Gone, vanished into thin air. They went out last night to work a surveillance and never came back." The agent cleared his throat. "I borrowed a page from your war book, Belasko. I went way out of bounds, but I used my badge and flexed some muscle at their bank. Their accounts are well into the six figures. I also staked out their homes. Both guys have brand-new cars, one a Jaguar, the other a Mercedes. It looks like they've even got a yacht down at the marina. I know, you were right. It kills me to say that. But we'll find them."

"If they're even still alive," Bolan said.

Tasker and Brockton were silent for a long moment, then looked grimly aware of that possibility, or angered that two of their own looked dirty. Then Tasker said, "Like you implied, Belasko, you want to be on hand for the seizure of all time, you're free to tag along."

"I think I'll skip it."

"Then maybe you might just want to skip right out of town," Brockton added.

Bolan showed both agents an easy smile. "No, I think I'll hang around. Maybe go down to the beach, relax, sip a piña colada, just enjoy the day."

Brockton snorted, and both agents stared with suspicion at Bolan for several moments. Then, without another word, they went back to their car. Bolan waited until they were backing out of the alley before he slid into the war wagon. His next stop was either going to bring some concrete answers, or the kind of trouble that might have it all blow up in Bolan's face.

"WE'VE GOT TO STOP meeting like this, Johnny," Waters told Bolan. "And that's not meant as any cliché or some attempt to be funny."

The Executioner believed it. He took a seat in the booth across from Waters. Bolan saw the man was highly agitated, frightened. Two empty shot glasses and two beer mugs, likewise drained, told Bolan the man was on his way for a nasty binge, but just trying to hold himself together.

"What have you got?" Bolan said, giving the bar a hard search, seeing a few barflys, three waitresses on duty and scattered groups of men and women.

Two pool tables were occupied by young guys who didn't look anything like Mafia. But Bolan wasn't trusting surface appearances. His van was parked outside in a packed lot, front end against a concrete wall. He was playing everything close to the edge, just like the enemy.

Bolan looked at Waters. Rock music was playing on the jukebox, allowing them to speak in normal tones. He ordered coffee when the waitress came, and Waters asked for another beer and another shot of whiskey.

"Take it easy on that stuff," Bolan suggested.

"Take it easy, right," Waters said. "I just sent the four semis to the hangar. Tartaglia's men are crawling all over the place, guarding the other truck. Relaxed is the last thing I feel. I had to sneak out. I can't be gone long."

"They suspect anything after what happened last night?"

"They suspect everybody. Here's what you wanted to know. They said the shipment is in and ready to be loaded, pronto. Right where I said it'd be. I can't say exactly when they'll be hauling it, but my guess, with all the guns the Don will be sending, it'll probably be tonight, after the rush hour. It's going to be a damn convoy, an armed convoy. Five trucks, rolling up I-95. The way it looks, I figure each semi will be holding anywhere from a ton to two tons. The way his soldiers were scrambling around, they're loading every last brick of dope Tartaglia has stashed in South Florida. Okay, the shipping orders that go with their final destinations are like this. Staggered convoy, once they get to the interchange near Jacksonville. Two go north for New York, the other three go west on Interstate 10. Houston, Chicago and Phoenix.''

''You're sure about this?'' Bolan said, then he told Waters about what he'd learned from Tasker about the container ship that was going to be raided.

Waters fell silent, as the waitress brought the coffee, beer and shot. The man worked on his beer, killed the whiskey, then looked around.

''Now you told me that, I'm more positive than ever,'' Waters said, firing up a cigarette with a trembling hand. ''That container ship is a decoy. All available law enforcement is going to be tied up, going through that ship, stem to stern, top to bottom. That's the whole idea. But that's the way it goes with a major load, especially if the mover knows he's hot. He leaks it out about a decoy vessel, ship, plane, truck whatever, maybe over a phone that's hot, or through an informant. I've even done it for Tartaglia in the past, just in case. But the real thing is happening now, just the way I told you.''

Bolan nodded, thinking about the convoy. ''Shouldn't be too hard tracking a convoy of five semis.''

Waters chuckled. ''It'll be a piece of cake. The Family calls their citrus company, get this, Happy Citrus. On the sides of the semis you've got an orange with a happy face. I don't know what you've got planned, I don't even want to know, but you'd have to be blind to miss those trucks.''

Bolan knew Waters was too scared to not be telling him the truth or even setting him up to be hit. It looked like the Executioner was in, along with his air firepower support from Grimaldi, for a war on the interstate. Bolan intended to see that convoy never reached Jacksonville. If they moved late at night, traffic would be light, which was a definite plus in keeping innocent travelers out of the firing line of a rolling war zone. It would be as near perfect a killing zone as Bolan and Grimaldi could hope for. Still, it was going to be tough.

"Look, I'm going back to work, but I can feel the strain, pal."

"Just carry on like it's another day," Bolan suggested. "Hold tough, you're almost clear. Which brings me to something we need to talk about."

"How come I don't like the sound of that?"

"You have friends or relatives who live out of town?"

"Yeah. My wife has a family outside Atlanta. What are you telling me? Tartaglia's going to come gunning for me? Hit my family?"

"Not if I can help it, Waters. Look, get yourself together. When I leave here, there's a good chance you're never going to see me again."

Fear came to the man's eyes. "How come I'm not all too reassured by that?"

"You're not on your own. By tomorrow morning, I can promise you'll never have to worry about looking over your shoulder for Tartaglia, any of his soldiers or the Rodrigos ever again. Use that beeper number. An Agent Tasker will call you back. I'll let him know about your situation."

"You mean I've got to come clean with my wife after I tell her I've entered a Witness Protection Program?"

"There's no other way, Waters. You wanted a second chance. I've done the best thing for you that can be done. This is it. The one-time offer."

Waters seemed to collapse inside himself. He drew a deep breath and seemed to steel himself after long moments of hard thought. He looked Bolan in the eye, resigned to his fate. "You're right, friend. Maybe that's the best way."

"It's the only way." Bolan tossed some money on the table and headed for the door.

12

They might have duped the DEA, but the tentacles of the narcotics hydra were all gathered, ready to be severed and crushed by the Executioner.

Only Bolan faced two immediate problems, one of which urged him to step up his timetable while the other predicament had him holding out for a viable alternative.

First, time was running out on the campaign. The DEA, the Coast Guard and other law-enforcement officials would go through that container ship, leave no panel or floorboard unchecked, and it would eat up their own time. That alone could help Bolan stretch his stakeout, then trackdown and total eradication of the enemy, but only up to a point. Once the good guys discovered the Rodrigos had sent them on the proverbial wild-goose chase, Tasker would waste no time picking it up a notch. If Bolan crossed paths with the DEA Organized Crime Task Force again, and this time with egg all over their face, he could be confronted and issued all kinds of ultimatums. In short, Tasker would do his damnedest to shut down Agents Belasko and Griswald, send them packing back to Washington. As it stood, it was going to be a major headache anyway for the DEA to make the Justice Department's "unofficial covert action" against the narcotraffickers go away without a trace. Brognola would do everything in his power to make sure Bolan and Grimaldi stayed on-line, then vanished once the campaign was finished.

That was the future, and Bolan was only concerned now with the present. A grim realist, the soldier knew the future was always in doubt.

The second problem to be solved was that there were enough gunmen, in and around the giant hangar, that Bolan knew he could only decimate their numbers with air firepower support. The problem there was that some of the enemy would escape if they came under sudden, even overwhelming firepower. Indeed, Bolan figured the hardmen would scatter all over town, head for airports, or maybe just crank up the engines on fifty-foot cabin cruisers and head out to sea.

He considered radioing Grimaldi to get the man there ASAP, but being so close to Homestead Air Force Base and the city of Miami could present sticky interference that might force Stony Man's top ace to ground his copter once his guns started blazing. Official red tape haggling at this late stage would handcuff both of them, and blow the search-and-destroy.

Bolan decided to hold out for the one option he knew he'd eventually take. And that was all-out warfare on the open highway.

Surveillance, wait, then dog the convoy whenever

it started rolling. Once on the interstate, he'd search for the critical opening where he and Grimaldi could deliver the most crushing blow.

Earlier, the Executioner had parked the war wagon near an abandoned quarry, a quarter mile west. The Beretta and Desert Eagle were in place beneath his dark windbreaker as he'd hunched low, crept closer to the enemy marks while winding his way through the tall weeds and sawgrass. He found a position near a gulley where he crouched in the brush. The enemy was right then maybe a hundred yards east. Even with the sun setting and at his back, Bolan didn't want to risk getting any closer.

He gave his surroundings another hard surveillance, combat senses on full alert for any sign of movement around him. There was a runway, south of the hangar, but Bolan could only spot a few twin-engine aircrafts parked at the far eastern edge, near a series of smaller hangars. Other than all the activity around the targeted hangar, Bolan thought the place could've been abandoned.

Far to his right flank, there was a junkyard of stripped-down planes, toppled fuel drums, strewed tires and other discarded equipment. The perimeter around the giant hangar was open ground, and only one main road led to the highway. It was from that direction Bolan caught the last of the semis rolling in an hour earlier. The doors on the hangar electronically opened, and through his high-powered field glasses Bolan had seen the other tractor trailers, lined up inside a hangar that could easily house perhaps ten transport planes.

The major players were all gathered, he saw again looking through his binos. Even the bikers. There was some connection between the Devil's Horsemen, the Mafia and the Colombians, but what, Bolan couldn't even guess. It didn't matter. The biker gang was going down hard, just like the rest, Bolan determined.

Tartaglia and the Rodrigos had disappeared inside the hangar. At least three dozen vehicles were parked around the hangar. They ranged in everything from vans to luxury cars. Soldiers, either belonging to the Rodrigos or Tartaglia, were patrolling the hangar's perimeter, or constantly moved, in and out of doors on both sides of the structure. It almost seemed to Bolan they didn't have a care in the world that they might be under surveillance, strolling around, armed to the teeth.

Well, the Executioner was more determined than ever that he would, and when he did, they'd know it. In fact, it would be the last thing they ever knew.

Suddenly, Bolan heard tires crunching debris. Snapping his head left, going lower and barely able to see through the weeds and saw grass, he spotted the black sedan. Had he been spotted? Or was it a crew of hardmen simply giving the area a recon?

Adrenaline racing, he drew the Beretta, threaded the sound suppressor on the muzzle and slowly dropped to the ground. As he heard the engine rumble past his position, Bolan rolled down the incline, found a steel pipe in the gulley and hid behind it. A moment later, car doors opened.

Bolan braced himself for the worst. He lifted the

Beretta, finger curling around the trigger. Even if he was forced to take out a recon party, it would alert every last gunman at the hangar.

The soldier heard footsteps crunching over debris, heading his way.

STILES WAS GETTING impatient. Sitting there on his Harley, chain-smoking and exchanging angry looks with his men, every second of every minute they malingered in front of the hangar frayed his nerves and stretched his mounting paranoia. Where were the big shots? he wondered. Inside, sure, but how long did it take to load five semis? Was there a problem? Were they plotting something against him? Were they cutting him out? Were they going to step through the doors and give the order to all these hard guys to kill them?

Stiles gave the area around the hangar a hard look. He figured it was impossible to get an accurate fix on how many gunmen he was looking at, and might have to take on if it went sour. It was a gangster fashion show, he thought, a jewelry convention, a sunglasses exhibition. Nothing but silk, gold, diamonds, python and alligator skin all around him. And a whole lot of guns. One big happy drug family. If nothing else, Stiles gave these guys some begrudging respect for wearing themselves for exactly what they were. And that was the biggest of the bigtime players. The kind of attitude he understood.

It was getting late in the day. Stiles needed to get on the handheld radio, get a plan worked out with his men back at the compound. If something fell through now, they'd roll into Miami and start wasting both Tartaglia's people and the Rodrigo bunch. But Stiles didn't think it would come to that, or maybe he was clinging to fading hope that his part of the deal would work out. These guys were going all the way, playing for keeps and they wanted those loads out of state, quick. But when? Any longer hanging around, and nightfall was going to drop over them. Maybe that was the idea. A run up the interstate under the cover of darkness, but he'd seen the trucks, with their big happy face orange on the sides. The Don might as well tell the world who he was.

An electronic whir sounded, and Stiles saw the hangar doors part just enough for the big shots to slip through. More silk and dark shades. Tartaglia was scowling, surrounded by his gunmen as he headed for his sedan. The Rodrigo brothers walked toward Stiles, who felt his heart beat faster.

"Here it is, amigo," Fernando Rodrigo said. "Listen to me very carefully, don't speak, don't object."

One of the gunmen walked up to Stiles and held out a piece of paper. Stiles saw an address on the slip of paper as he took it from the hardman.

Fernando Rodrigo fired up a cigarette. "That's an address on Bourbon Street. That's right, you're going to New Orleans with one of the trucks. The man you'll contact is named Alvarez. What you'll do, is, you'll stay in New Orleans. Take or have one hundred kilos of my product brought to you there. You'll have one week to prove to me you can move it. When you return you'll have my money and the rest of my product. Depending on how it goes with you, I'll decide whether we can do business. I warn you. You won't fail to deliver to me what I'm asking for. I'm no longer prepared to continue fucking around with you."

The Don spoke up. "Don't you think for a second I like this. You stay a good distance back of my trucks. Something goes wrong, I'll come for you and you'll die slowly and in great pain."

Stiles was in, and that was all he needed to know. Too much was riding on the line for the big shots, he knew, for them to even consider some grandstand suicide move right then. Already Stiles was putting his own moves together. As soon as he was out of sight, he'd contact his compound, have twenty-five men ready to file in behind him at a Fort Lauderdale exit. Of course, he wouldn't bring the first brick to New Orleans until he checked out the setup. But things sure sounded promising. Sweet, even.

"You listening to what I'm saying, one-percenter?" Tartaglia growled. "You fuck this up, it'd be better if you went ahead and plowed your bike into a telephone pole at a hundred miles an hour than have to deal with me."

"Relax, Godfather," Stiles said, showing the man a grin. "All we wanted was a little piece of the action. Everything is going to be beautiful, man."

Tartaglia barked at the soldier near him to get him the hell out of there. Moments later, the Don and three of his soldiers had piled into the sedan, and the vehicle's tires were spitting up dust as the wheel-man roared out of there.

"Memorize that address, then burn it," Juan Carlos Rodrigo said.

Stiles flicked open his lighter and put a flame to the paper. "Consider it done."

"Wait at the end of this road," the older brother ordered. "You'll know when it is underway."

They spun on their heels, the brothers disappearing back into the hangar.

Stiles grinned at his men, then cranked on his engine. "It's show time, brothers."

The outlaw biker leader felt confident, but he was going to stay cautious. He didn't think he cared too much for the Don talking down to him like that, as if he were some punk. Maybe when he was climbing the ladder of the coke world, getting his start in New Orleans, he'd return to Miami and let the Don know just how little he really cared for being threatened.

Stiles had visions of walking right into the godfather's estate and slapping the old man around before he stuck a knife into his gut. Then he could tell the Rodrigos some story about how the Don was planning to cut them out of the picture, take over their entire distribution network. Then he'd work an angle on getting rid of the Rodrigos. There were plenty of dealers in town.

Stiles hit the throttle and thundered into the wind. The future held all kinds of possibilities.

BOLAN HEARD THE FOOTSTEPS, closing over his position, then they stopped. In the distance, he then caught the sound of thunder. Engines were roaring to life, and he recognized the sound of the Harleys.

"Ain't nothing out here, Paulie," Bolan heard a man growl. Close. Too close. The soldier didn't trust the moment at all. If they spotted the weeds and grass matted down, they'd know someone had been there.

"Boss said to check the area, we check it," another man said, a voice that was almost right overtop of Bolan.

The Executioner remained motionless. He stayed perched near the pipe, Beretta in hand, looking up. Finally, he chanced moving around, angling his body in the direction of the voices as they bickered back and forth about getting out of there and back to the hangar.

Then Bolan heard them clomping around in the junkyard, the sounds of men angrily kicking things, tossing objects aside. He looked at his chronometer after an agonizing eternity of waiting for them to eventually spot his place of concealment.

Thirty minutes had passed. The sun sank behind the trees to the west.

Finally, car doors slammed and Bolan heard the sedan's engine roar to life. Tires grabbed at the earth above him, spewing a funnel of dust over his position.

Bolan waited. It could be they were ready to spring one of the oldest ploys known to flush out a suspected enemy in hiding. The car would drive off, and the hidden man was supposed to believe they were gone. Only they had left behind a waiting gun.

So the Executioner gave it another half hour, straining his senses, knowing that any soldier who might have been left behind couldn't stay still that long, remain that quiet.

Beretta poised to fire, Bolan finally eased out of the gulley.

They had left, or so it appeared, but he checked the junkyard just the same. The search was time-consuming. He stayed low, vigilance on the hangar and the junkyard. The long shadows stretching over him helped blanket his movements.

Satisfied they were indeed gone, Bolan returned to his original surveillance spot near the gulley.

Time crept by. The sun vanished; darkness fell.

Bolan needed to touch base with Grimaldi. Still no semis emerged from the hangar.

Then the doors opened in the distance, and Bolan heard the crank and grind of diesel engines firing up.

They were moving.

Shadows were piling into the vehicles, as one by one the semis lumbered out of the hangar.

GRIMALDI HAD SWEATED out the day, waiting to hear from Bolan. Why hadn't he called? A thousand-and-one scenarios, all of them bad, wanted to nag their way into Grimaldi's mind. But he knew the big man. The situation was under control.

The ace pilot paced around the gunship, the warbird a big dark silhouette in the clearing now that nightfall had enveloped the base.

Maybe no news was good news, he decided, sipping on his tenth cup of coffee.

The radio in the gunship suddenly crackled. Grimaldi was through the fuselage doorway in an eyeblink, sweeping into the cockpit as he heard the familiar voice say, "S-Force to G-Force, come in, G-Force."

Grimaldi slipped on his radio headset. "G-Force here. What's the situation?"

"They're rolling. Standby but get it cranked up and ready to liftoff. I'll get back to you. We're on, G-Force. Stay hard."

Bolan signed off. It was a go.

Lock, load and lift off.

Grimaldi settled into the cockpit seat, feeling his adrenaline racing.

It was time to rock and roll.

13

With his heart pounding hard enough to nearly buckle his knees from knifing chest pains, Tartaglia strode across the patio of his estate, poured a stiff Scotch whiskey in a glass at the poolside bar, then stared out across the infinite blackness of the Atlantic Ocean. He wasn't going to sleep that night, he knew, but no one was going to catch even a half hour of shut-eye on the Palm Beach compound. Not on his watch.

Not when his whole kingdom, a multibillion-dollar empire, was threatened to be crushed to ruins.

He sipped his drink, then fired up a foot-long Havana cigar. Looking out to sea, thoughts of his father wanted to creep into his mind. But this was no time for nostalgia or feeling sentimental. This was the eleventh hour of absolute and dire crisis, as terrifying and nerve-racking as it could get, where it was hit or miss, and missing meant he was dead. All he knew was that his father would have expected nothing short of his son standing up, taking it on the chin, if necessary, but fighting it out to the bitter end, even if it meant dying to protect what was his.

Puffing on his cigar, the whiskey warming his

belly, he listened to the gentle break of the waves on the beach and strained his ears to catch any sound that was out of the ordinary. Silence. Or did he hear voices, coming from down the beach? Was that a shadow he saw down by his dock? He'd have someone check it out.

The compound was on full alert. His soldiers numbered twelve on the compound, half on the beach or around the pool, three inside, three out front. Naturally, he had sent his best people on the run, but he had no choice. This wasn't a time to cut corners, walk on tiptoes. Either way, his men there were armed to the teeth, a couple of guys monitoring banks of screens, cameras that watched the compound on all points of the compass. He hoped it would be enough, the guns and the cameras. If anything was out of the ordinary, they were under orders to shoot first, ask questions later.

A thorough check of the block, and his soldiers had informed him there were no cops or DEA staking out the compound. The whole place had been swept for bugs, phones checked by his electronics people, twice. Clean. It sounded good, sure enough, too good, since his place was usually under twenty-four-hour surveillance by the DEA. No, he couldn't trust a damn thing right then, couldn't afford to believe in anyone other than perhaps his soldiers, himself, and his own brother. Even still, everyone was suspect, both blood and trusted soldiers alike.

He had survived in this business long enough to know everyone and anyone would lie or set the other guy up to save his own skin. Before now, leaks had always been found, plugged right away, with a bullet, or a meat hook that hung some guy up by his heels while his flesh was skinned off him, piece by piece. This time, though, something else was happening, some human storm he sensed, out there in the night, prepared to blow his way and rip his whole world apart.

Through a break in the wall of the palm trees, he glimpsed his cabin cruiser, tied to the dock. He considered taking a ride out to sea for a little while until he received the only news he wanted to hear.

But he wouldn't hear anything until late tomorrow. Just to get the convoy to Jacksonville, up I-95, to the interchange was almost two hundred miles. Hell, just the waiting to hear positive news was going to send his blood pressure soaring.

And the tonnage alone was enough to keep his blood racing with fear, no, pure terror, given all that had happened. And the money he had shelled out, in both cash and wire transfers? He had heard the sum from his accountants and his counsel, all of whom he was keeping on hand, within eyeshot, in the living room of his estate. It was a staggering amount, and only he and his closest associates knew the figures—155 million, and change.

Put together with the Rodrigo load, complete with five hundred kilos of uncut heroin—almost every last brick he had left on hand in Miami—and those semis were hauling a combined twenty-two tons of product. That didn't even include another thirty million he had promised the Rodrigos, who had fronted him close to another ton, in good faith, once he had proved he had the money on hand, that it was only a matter of a week before he could get the rest of it together. The Cali brothers had been so anxious to do the deal, they were willing to stretch themselves, take the risk. Naturally, some interest was involved on the front end, but it was mere pennies compared to the whole deal.

The Don made another drink. If anything went wrong on that run, he was finished. At least for a long, long time. He would have to take a vacation, somewhere far away, guarded around-the-clock. Chicago, New York and Houston had already paid upfront for their merchandise. If it didn't get there, they would send some people to Miami to have a little talk with him. That was only one of several worst-case scenarios.

And now this business with the bikers. Not good. But like other crisis situations, he had very little choice but to roll the dice. His whole world was either going to expand and make him the richest trafficker in the country, or it was all going to come crashing down. He was going for broke this time, scrambling to save his empire, hanging everything he had out there to be chopped off.

The Don called across the pool to one of his soldiers. "Joey, bring my two boys out here."

Tartaglia waited while Joey Pazolli went to round up his DEA people—Wilkins and Johnson, one white, one black, both of them one year bought and paid for. They were special agents of that new Organized Crime Task Force. It was time to sweat them a little, Tartaglia thought.

Then there was Parker, the lawyer who handled a lot of the business, who had the necessary contacts in overseas banking, and mapped out a lot of the logistics in the money-moving, the cleaning of drug money. Something didn't feel right with his counsel and that business at his home the past night. With everything that was happening, there'd been no time to feel Parker out. Yeah, the guy wasn't telling him everything he knew about these two so-called home invaders, Tartaglia decided.

Later, the Don figured it was best to strap on the Colt .45 pistol he had in his study. He picked up the portable phone, then went to sit in a thick-cushioned chair in the cabana. He hadn't spoken to his brother since this whole fiasco had started. Another drink to calm his nerves, and he would touch base with Sal. At a time like this, a man needed to be close to family.

Tartaglia watched as the two agents strolled across the patio, walking across the deck, not a worry in the world. They even had drinks in hand, cigars in their mouths. Tartaglia felt his blood boil. These salt-and-pepper badges in his pocket were taking advantage of his generosity and good nature, especially when they made a beeline for the bar to freshen up their drinks. Making him wait on them. They had been disarmed of their Glock pistols, but they still acted like they could handle anything that came their way. Time to get some things straight here. Finally, they sauntered into the cabana.

Tartaglia's gaze narrowed, as he puffed on his cigar. Two soldiers, with mini-Uzis slung around their shoulders, were perched near the bar. Wilkins and Johnson sat across the table from the Don.

"I want to tell you two scumbags something, and you listen good or I'll sink your feet in a concrete block and drop you in my own pool," Tartaglia began, an edge in his voice. The agents stiffened with anger and resentment in their eyes. "Good. I see I got your full attention. Now. You're walking around here like you own the place, my place, my home for almost twenty years, smoking my cigars, drinking my booze. You're on my payroll, taking my money. You're in my home, and you'll show respect. Next time you want a drink, you ask me if you can have one. Do we understand each other?"

They looked set to comment, flex some muscle even, but Wilkins and Johnson exchanged a nervous look, their clean-scrubbed and lean faces showing strain.

"Understood," Wilkins said. "I apologize."

"How about you, boy?" the Don growled at the black agent. "That's right, I called you 'boy.' Your move. Call it. You don't think this old man can rip your black throat out with his bare hands? You stand up and try me on for size."

For a second, Tartaglia thought Johnson was going to get some attitude, then the agent glanced over his shoulder at the hardmen and turned to stare with pure hatred at the Don, but didn't move. Obviously, the Don thought, Johnson seemed to think better of it, a guy considering his future and all that, and Don Paolo nodded.

"Now, here's what I've got," the Don said. "I

don't give a shit if you were picked up by my men without warning. Way I heard it from you, your own people know you're dirty. Sounds like my men snatching you up was the best thing could have happened to you. You even tell me you saw they had your houses staked out. Your boss even came out of your banks like he's seen a ghost. I did some checking myself and found out you two are living as big as I do. Flashing yourselves all over town, like you own something, like you're in charge of your lives. I ask myself, has this been going on for a year now? Christ, could it be these two assholes are why I'm so hot all of a sudden.'' They squirmed, and the Don blew a cloud of smoke in their faces. ''I put money in your pockets, over a million in cash, last time I checked, and you're out there, eating surf and turf every night, got wheels and boats that scream you're as dirty as a tub of shit. Looking you both in the eye now, and I tell you that's over, the good times, the high times, kiss it goodbye. You're with me until I say otherwise. My fate is your fate.''

Wilkins cleared his throat. ''Uh, that's something we need to discuss.''

''What's to discuss? Something gets fucked on my end, I'm coming right to you.''

''Everything will hold,'' Johnson said.

''Will it? So far, everything's been falling apart. And to tell you the truth, I don't feel like I'm getting my money's worth anymore.''

Sweat beaded on Wilkins's forehead. ''We need to get out of the country. If they get to us, I don't even want to think about what could happen.''

"Fuck that!" Tartaglia snarled. "I don't want to hear about your petty problems. Stop whining! You came to me, not the other way around. Tell me I got nothing to worry about here."

Wilkins hit his drink and got himself composed enough to speak. "Look, all I'm saying is that we're hot, and they know it. If we even try to take out our money, they'll drop a net over us."

"We're all hot!" the Don raged, slamming his fist on the table, fighting off the smile as he saw them flinch. "That net is right over my head and ready to drop. You got any idea how my whole life is on the line with this run? You know how much planning, how much sweat and fear, how much money I've dumped into this deal? No, of course not, you just sit back and feed me a little information about phone taps and surveillance and take my hard-earned money. Of course, the mere fact that you've been able to hold out so long tells me the heat I face isn't all that smart. Me, I can smell you two clear across town. Okay, here it is, gentlemen," the Don snarled with contempt in his voice. "You get the hell out of my face, go inside and wait for me. Next time we talk, you damn well better have something for me."

Now they were both sweating, Tartaglia saw. Good. Something of a small victory in what had so far been a string of defeats and disasters. They'd have something for him. He'd know every last detail of any operation of this special task force that could be possibly mounted against him, or they would be floating at the bottom of his pool. They both killed their drinks. Tartaglia felt a thin smile stretch his lips. They knew they'd better come through, or else.

"Yeah, go on, make yourselves another one," the Don said.

He waited until they went to the bar, fixed themselves a drink and were escorted back inside the mansion by one of his soldiers.

Then the Don called his brother. Two rings, and he heard the voice of one of his brother's men answer.

"Let me talk to Sal."

The man didn't have to ask who it was, but Tartaglia knew he'd have to wait for his brother to get to the phone. For years, the two of them had run the business, brothers, just like the Rodrigos. When Sal had fallen too ill to even venture outside his West Palm home, Don Paolo had been forced to pick up his brother's end. The Don felt his heart grow heavy with sorrow and regret. He could just see his brother, shuffling for the phone now, so frail and withered a gentle breeze could blow him over. These days, Sal just sat around the pool, pumped with pain pills and booze, and yes, even some coke. Tartaglia had to wonder where it had all gone so wrong.

A croaking voice came on the line. "Yeah."

"Sal, it's your brother."

"Yeah, hey, good to hear from you, Paulie," Sal wheezed. "Been wondering, hell, been worried sick about you. Heard about what's been happening. You got things under control, I hope."

The Don felt the lie twist a white-hot dagger in his belly, even as it formed on his tongue. "Everything's under control, Sal. There's problems, but I'm working on it. How are you feeling?''

"The usual. Walking death.''

The Don heaved a breath. "Listen, how much security have you got?''

"Six guys. Plus I'm keeping my own piece, right on me.''

"Should I send a couple extra guys over?''

"Nah. Everything will be fine here. Listen, you hold tough. We've been through bad as this before.''

But never this close to the edge, Tartaglia thought. He kept up putting on the positive spin. "We'll make it. When this is done, Sal, me and you, we'll sit down and take a look at things.''

Sal Tartaglia chuckled, a gravelly voice that seemed to hit Don Paolo's ears from the bottom of a tomb. "You need to take a vacation. I'm all for that. Need to get out of this town anyway.''

"You got it, Sal. Listen, get some rest. I didn't mean to make myself so scarce these past couple of days. I'll be in touch later.''

The Don hung up on his brother. He couldn't take it any longer, hearing that voice, riddled with pain and that undertone of fear, a dying soul clinging desperately to life. It was cutting way too close to his own home.

AT FORT LAUDERDALE, Bolan had seen the bikers hit I-95, a small army of motorcycles, streaking up the on-ramp, linking up with the other club members he'd seen at the hangar.

There were about three dozen Devil's Horsemen

in all now, strung out in the right lane, falling in behind the convoy. Lining the roadway were the one van the bikers had, five of the Don's luxury wheels, then next in line, rolling point, the five semis. It was enough to let Bolan know that, with or without Grimaldi, it was going to be hard from there on. Luckily, the farther Bolan drove north, traffic thinned, any vehicles of innocent and nonsuspecting travelers almost nonexistent at that late hour. Once they cleared each major exit on the way north, the dark countryside became more and more shrouded in isolation, black sentinels of prehistoric-looking vegetation looming beyond the shoulders, in both the north and southbound lanes.

Hands wrapped around the steering wheel of the war wagon, Bolan was now rolling past Palm Beach. Forget the swank and exclusive mansions to the east. The Executioner had tunnel vision, fixed solely ahead on the staggered convoy.

Back at the hangar, he had given the convoy some lead, stayed at least three-quarters of a mile to their rear, once they made the interstate north of Miami. South, between Miami and Fort Lauderdale, it had taken a good thirty minutes for the convoy to get rolling, crank it up to sixty-five miles per hour as the vehicles linked up. Checking the speedometer, Bolan found the enemy hugging the speed limit at close to sixty-five mph.

It was time to raise Grimaldi for liftoff.

14

Something was wrong. One minute Michael Palazzi was monitoring the CB, hooked to the dashboard of the sedan, and the next second there was nothing but static. On all frequencies, including the state police band, it was the same thing. The hideous crackling noise warned him someone was either working overtime to intercept their own frequency, or they were jammed. In effect, they were cut off from one another and from intercepting other radio messages. Ground control was gone.

The wheelman, Paulie Moran, shot Palazzi a worried look. "What's the matter?"

Snapping off the CB, Palazzi twisted in his seat, looking past Bartone and Stanelli. Both soldiers in the back seat followed Palazzi's grim stare to their rear.

The bikers were strung out in the right lane, a long column of Harleys and one van, maybe a quarter mile behind the sedan, a lot closer than the Don would have appreciated. All in all, it now looked like a possible worst-case scenario. Everything was packed, the whole convoy locked on a roll. Damn it. Sitting ducks. And Palazzi's own vehicle picked up the rear of the Don's trailing hardforce, their wheels pinched in, pretty tight at that speed, between the bikers and their own crew. Four vehicles, two Cadillacs, a Lexus and another sedan were ahead of Palazzi's wheels, with the convoy of semis, lumbering through the night, in a line, another quarter to maybe a half mile ahead of his position.

Nowhere to go. Suddenly it all looked and felt bad. And it was still a long way to Jacksonville. He told himself to hold on, don't panic.

"You want to try it again?" Bartone asked.

Stanelli cursed the bikers, trying to will them out of the way so he could get a better look.

Palazzi ignored the soldiers. There was virtually no traffic behind the bikers. But he peered hard beyond the small army of bikers and picked out the bulky shape of some vehicle, coming up hard on the Devil's Horsemen. It looked like a van, a big van.

Trouble was about to hit them; he was sure of it. Fifteen years as Don Paolo's top and most trusted lieutenant, and Palazzi had seen enough trouble to recognize a hit about to happen when he saw one. Twenty-two tons of narcotics or not, their lives were on the line. Suddenly, the load didn't mean all that much, not if they were dead. "I want to drop back behind those bikers. Hit the shoulder, but easy, and keep it rolling," Palazzi ordered his wheelman. "Fellas, break out the hardware."

They didn't have to be told twice. A compartment was built into the back seat, between his soldiers. Bartone opened the cushioned slat, reached through, hauled out three Uzi submachine guns and passed them out. Palazzi was checking the clip, cocking the bolt action when something suddenly caught his eye to the west.

Something was flying over the trees beyond the southbound lane.

Palazzi felt his heart race. Not now, he heard his mind silently rage. They were being tracked by air and ground.

"Roll down the window, Paulie," Palazzi growled, wanting to hear something that would confirm it was, in fact, a chopper he saw.

The skilled wheelman hit a button to electronically roll down his window even as he slowed the sedan, sliding onto the shoulder. Hot air rushed through the interior. Palazzi strained his ears and eyes, looking west at the big object soaring over the trees. A distant sound confirmed his worst fear.

And the chopper was flying parallel with the convoy. They were being hit.

"Keep it on the shoulder, Paulie. Stanelli, wave those biker assholes past us. See that van back there? I want to get a good look at the driver. If anything doesn't look right, I give the word, we cut loose."

Grimly, they nodded in response to Palazzi's order. Stanelli waved the bikers past as the sedan slowed and Moran kept it on the shoulder.

The black van closed, and Palazzi caught a glimpse of the driver. He didn't know how he knew, but he had a description from the Don about one of the bastards who had been hitting them so hard.

Palazzi felt his finger curl around the Uzi's trigger

as he watched the black van close, rocket ahead, then cut the gap to their position.

WIND HAMMERING HIM in the face, his eyes shielded by goggles, Stiles saw the last of the Don's vehicles in the five-car crew slide onto the shoulder and wave them past. Stiles had long since spotted the big van on their rear, having picked them up way back at Fort Lauderdale. They were marked, he knew, and they were going to be hit. And none of the semis looked ready to slow down or pull over. Stiles got the picture. The only thing that was going to stop the Don's crew was death.

The biker leader opened his satchel and pulled out the Heckler & Koch MP-5 subgun, already cocked and locked. It would be tricky, firing on the fly, into the wind at sixty-five mph, one hand on the throttle. He didn't see any other way.

Then, to the north, he spotted the helicopter. It was flying low and hard, ahead of the column of semis. Then the bird veered, banked and hovered over the southbound lane, maybe two miles ahead of the lead semi, a distant black speck against the veil of night. It was setting up the convoy from that distant point of interception, a waiting bird of prey.

Stiles lifted his submachine gun and waved it to let the others know to draw their own hardware. They were on full alert.

He was checking his sideview mirror when he saw the black van swing out into the far left lane. The black van! The guy back in Miami. The big guy with the hand cannon, eyes of steel, a no-shit way about him. Stiles could see his face, set like a death mask, behind the wheel as the guy hit the gas and sent the van like a missile, streaking up on their rear.

A plan formed in the biker leader's mind. Survival.

Stiles would hang back, sending the others ahead once the van surged past. Depending on what happened, he'd either keep riding, or stop and head back for the compound. He still had enough cocaine to save his own world. The Cali brothers and the Don could kiss his one-percent ass goodbye. No way was he giving up what he had worked, sweated and nearly died for to get.

Stiles didn't have to wait much longer to find out what was going to happen. He watched the side door of the van open. A moment later, something came protruding from the interior on a long metallic arm.

Stiles cursed, as he saw the machine-gun flame, cut loose on the sedan that had dropped behind his column.

Call it instinct, fear, whatever, but Stiles knew they were all screwed.

THEY WERE GOING to save the load or they were going down and staying down, scattered and spread all over I-95, in bits and pieces of flesh mingled with flaming wreckage. As far as Bolan was concerned, that was the only play he wanted. The enemy wasn't going back to Miami, nor were they going to get much farther down the road.

Ten minutes earlier, Grimaldi had patched

through. "Their eggs are scrambled, Sarge. Your move."

It was a key to whatever success they would seize, Bolan knew. The gunship was equipped with a state-of-the-art "Quick Fix" system. Grimaldi had located the radio frequency of the convoy and jammed it, and at the same time had most likely knocked out any state police bands. Time would run out before the state police screamed onto the interstate—and the timing of a coordinated ground-and-air assault was everything on this hit. If nothing else, Bolan was now able to freely communicate with his air fire support without the enemy knowing the next, and the final, move.

The other advantage was that once the convoy discovered it was cut off by radio, the gunners might panic, start searching the skies, their rear, and force a play that would launch the road war.

It had worked.

Ahead Bolan saw the last of the Don's vehicles swing onto the shoulder of the interstate. They were falling back to take a look at him. He knew he'd been spotted, glimpsing the muzzles of submachine guns as he closed on the sedan.

The Executioner took one of the three gunsticks, opened the side and the rear doors and swung over into the far lane. As the hot wind gusted through the interior, Bolan electronically extended the M-60 machine gun. The enemy didn't know it, but they had also given him the only chance to seal off the rear from any oncoming traffic. Grimaldi had already informed Bolan there was nothing ahead of the semis for a good two to three miles but open road.

It was as good as it was going to get. Patience was about to pay off. Once Bolan created some wreckage with the opening rounds of battle, though, all bets were off. And if the bikers attempted to cut him off, the Executioner would bulldoze and blaze his way through them. His objective was to get beyond the lead semi. There, he'd drop the mines while Grimaldi dumped his load of grenades and TOWs on any and everything that rode in the convoy.

One fell swoop, one titanic unleashing of Armageddon.

At least that was the plan. There was only one way to make it work, and that was to see it through.

Bolan patched through to Grimaldi. ''This is it, G-Force. I'm making my move now. Hold off. Next time you hear from me, I'll give you one word. 'Unload.'''

''That's affirmative, big guy. I'll hold my position. Right now, we're clear of any traffic to the north, for about two miles.''

After one last check of the gunship, spotting Grimaldi's warbird, hovering more than a mile to the north, Bolan came up on the lagging enemy vehicle and looked at the four hardmen inside the sedan. Two miles to work with.

The soldier glimpsed the fear on their faces, or maybe it was hate in their eyes as they thought they should recognize him. Whatever, a big gunner on the front passenger's side squeezed out the window, came up on the roof and started triggering his Uzi while another hardman in the rear did the same. If they had seen the M-60, they didn't seem to care.

In the next instant, Bolan made them wish they had chosen another line of work. Holding back on the gunstick's button, the Executioner stitched a lead hellstorm of 7.62 mm NATO slugs across the sedan, front to rear. The pounding gale force of Bolan's fire rocked the sedan, the lead sparking metal and shattering glass.

One hardforce was as good as dead.

Bolan fixed his deathsights on the biker army. Ahead, the Devil's Horsemen were twisted on their bikes, already hosing the van with autofire.

Bullets skidded off the passenger window and windshield. The glass began to crack, then the passenger window was shattered, giving way in a mini-explosion of shards and razoring slivers. Eyelids slit to mere cracks, a quick look in his side mirror showed Bolan the sedan hammering into the guardrail. There was a tremendous screech of metal on metal, then it burst into a ball of fire. Like some child's toy thrown by an angry child, the wreckage bounced off the rail and flipped back over the highway. That should cover the rear from oncoming traffic, and Bolan wanted to make certain all innocent travelers stayed put, well behind the rolling war zone.

Surging past the bikers, Bolan swept them with a long burst of machine-gun fire. Screams of agony meshed with the hot wind rushing in his ears. The van flew by the bikers as a half-dozen riders toppled and slammed to the pavement, broken to bursting sacks of blood on impact. There seemed to be a chain reaction of toppling, sliding and flying bodies, but Bolan saw that most of them held on, swerving past the wreckage and their sailing brothers. They were skilled riders, he knew, and suspected they were most likely pumped on adrenaline, fueled by fear and coke. In short, they were just as insane and hellbent on saving their world as the Don's crew.

More gunmen started poking out the windows of luxury vehicles as the soldier raced up on the Don's hardforce. The speedometer rose quickly before Bolan clipped 120 mph. The Executioner was grimly aware he had but split seconds to blaze past the semis and line up his targets for a ground-and-air attack.

In a blur, the Executioner was past the Don's hardforce before they could cut him off. Behind, he saw the bikers whip out into the passing lanes, their subguns flaming, bullets thudding into the hull behind Bolan, with a few wild shots slamming into the windshield.

The soldier took care of some of that deadly problem on his rear. A quick but lethal burst of cannon fire, and Bolan's line of 20 mm rounds tore through more of the Devil's Horsemen. Like small toys, shredded bodies were launched from their Harleys. Bikes slammed to the pavement, wreckage flying everywhere in screaming lines of sparking metal and bouncing bodies. Two, then three balls of fire mushroomed behind Bolan. More figures took to the air. Another burst of cannonfire decimated another of the Don's cars and sent it skybound on a thundering fireball.

Bolan made it past the lead truck and spotted Grimaldi swinging the chopper around, nose aimed at the convoy, which showed no signs of stopping. In fact, a glance in the passenger's sideview mirror and Bolan saw just how crazy the Don's crew was in its final savage hold to save the load.

Suddenly, one gunman was right on top of the cab of the lead semi, crouched and firing away with autofire from an assault rifle that was tracking Bolan.

It was too little too late for the enemy.

Bolan saw the army of bikers surging past the semis, subguns in hand.

The Executioner gauged the distance for the up-and-coming final blow.

Bolan patched through to Grimaldi as the soldier hit the button on the panel, releasing the whole load of Claymore mines.

"Unload."

15

With the moment of truth on hand, the Executioner gave the rear one last look, two heartbeats before he and G-Force dealt total and complete annihilation.

Devil's Horsemen were racing up the side of the convoy, firing their submachine guns in all directions.

The five semi trucks were rolling hard at sixty-five mph.

There was a gunner on the cab roof of the lead tractor trailer, crouched with his assault rifle stuttering and sweeping lead over the Executioner's vehicle.

Everything behind the soldier rolled, a long and thundering wave of man and machine, right over the mines, which were bouncing and dispersing all over the lead enemy numbers and vehicles.

Bolan punched the button and watched the mines explode.

In the next second, the helicopter's barrage of grenades and rockets started impacting at the front of the convoy and went thundering down the line from there.

Streaking earthbound were a couple dozen or

more 40 mm grenades. A few TOWs combined with the detonating mines, and the world shattered behind Bolan in a sudden blinding flash. Brilliant colors lit the night, screaming balls of fire appearing to take on a life of their own. Orange, white and even purple and red, it seemed, became living entities of giant mushrooming clouds, eating and sucking up everything in the swirling inferno. A tornado of fire then appeared to whorl down the length of the convoy as each semi took its turn being pounded by the helicopter's blanket of fiery wrath.

Even as he surged on, the first series of blasts were so tremendous, Bolan felt the van rock on its chassis. He fought to control the steering wheel, as the heat from the explosions screamed up so furious on the vehicle's rear that Bolan felt his face being scorched.

Behind him, forced to squint against the searing flashes, the Executioner saw bodies on Harleys hurled skyward, or launched clear across the median and into the southbound lane. Trailing screams of agony hit the air, bikers and whoever else on fire, incinerated by white phosphorous before they crunched to earth and skidded in torn and mangled bits and pieces. Huge slabs of flaming wreckage and chunks of asphalt whirled in all directions. Then more roaring balls of fire marched down the interstate.

It was too late for anyone to hit the brakes and save himself from certain death.

They were vaporized and hurtled for at least a hundred yards. Front to rear, Bolan saw Grimaldi was blanketing the enemy with not only death from above, but a vision of the Apocalypse.

The soldier kept driving, ready to cut loose with the 20 mm cannon should anything emerge from the fire that kept growing.

Nothing showed on Bolan's rear but a mini-holocaust as gas tanks, topped off, no doubt, before leaving Miami, ignited. One long screaming wall of fire after another meshed behind Bolan, shrieking out across the median for the woods and sky. It was such a perfectly timed and executed combined ground-and-air strike, it almost looked and felt too good to be true.

STILES HAD ALREADY suspected what was going to happen, maybe six critical seconds before it actually did. By the time he was hitting the brakes, most of his men were flying past him, going for the black van that was pounding out machine-gun and cannon fire. A quick look at the suspended chopper ahead, and Stiles had known the worst was ready to drop over the convoy.

The biker leader had swung his Harley around, cranking on the throttle, and rocketed back down the northbound lane, missiled it up to eighty, flying past the Don's cars, and going in the wrong direction when he looked behind and caught a vision of hell on earth.

Stiles raced into the wind. His only thought was to get back to the compound, snatch up his coke and get as far away from Florida as possible.

GRIMALDI FOUND HIMSELF mesmerized in a lingering second of dangerous fascination of the hell he had unleashed on the convoy. A good two hundred yards west of ground zero, he had poured the entire payload on the enemy, blanketed them, front to rear, with the most complete and horrific annihilation he believed he had ever seen.

But the firestorm he dropped on them was even a little more than he had expected. Working the collective and cyclic sticks, he was getting the helicopter away from the roaring wall of fire as fast as he could, ascending and banking with all the skill he could command. Everything down there was incinerated, on fire, ripped to sheer nothingness.

Banking back to the west, he spotted maybe a half-dozen bikers streaking down the interstate, going the wrong way, escaping the inferno.

Then the air shook around Grimaldi as the explosions kept thundering and screaming, and the incredible concussive force reached out to smack his gunship's hull.

Moments later, Grimaldi patched through to Bolan to get a fix on their next move. He didn't see how either of them could top what they had just wreaked, but he knew Bolan, and he knew this ultimate and final war against the narcotraffickers was just heating up.

BOLAN HAD FOUND the next exit and was racing down the ramp and into the southbound lane when Grimaldi came on the headset.

The pilot whistled softly in Bolan's ear. "How

come I get the feeling we just caught a glimpse of the end of the world?''

"Their world," the Executioner replied.

Skillfully, aware the clock could run out any second before the state police arrived on the scene, Bolan weaved his way past the onlookers. Delayed explosions belched in the distance. The soldier dodged a piece of raining debris and felt the road tremble behind him as he surged on. Grimaldi told him about the bikers and wanted to know their next play.

"How's your stock, G-Force?"

"I dumped the whole parade on them, Sarge."

"Ninety minutes until we link up. Reload at the base. I'm southbound. If you don't hear from me in ninety minutes, you're on your own." He gave Grimaldi the general area of the Rodrigo estate, but told him to find and hit the biker compound first. After, of course, the ace pilot re-armed the gunship. A quick sweep of the area Bolan believed where the bikers were fortressed and Grimaldi shouldn't have too much problem locating the Devil's Horsemen.

"How about the second target?" Grimaldi asked.

"Should be even easier to locate. Nothing but soldiers, I understand, patrolling the perimeter. It's the only estate in the area for ten blocks with more armed men than all of Miami PD."

Grimaldi confirmed his orders and signed off.

Gripping the steering wheel, Bolan plowed through some wreckage that barricaded the southbound lane. There was no stopping now. Next was Palm Beach.

The Executioner was going to make the Don the one and only offer that was in the cards.

THEY WERE RACING DOWN I-41, heading deep into Everglades country. Stiles was leading the charge through the swampland, his only thought to get to the compound.

He found he had only six men left. Time was critical and ticking away for Stiles to escape. Aware of only what was in front of him, the biker leader saw a dark shape, rumbling toward them. Then strobing lights from behind caught his attention. Turning, already knowing what he would find, the leader of the Devil's Horsemen saw two state police cruisers, streaking up on their rear, so hard and fast, they seemed to have come out of nowhere. He shouted the orders to his men. They knew what to do, the only thing they could do. They spread out in a staggered line, Stiles leading three of them across the opposite lane.

They drew their submachine guns and twisted and cut loose with their weapons on the cruisers. Screaming and cursing at the top of their lungs, Stiles and his men swept both vehicles with autofire, side to side, front to back. A horn blared ahead of Stiles. He screamed another curse, holding back on the SMG's trigger, blasting in the windshield of the lead cruiser. Metal sparked, and the glass caved on the trooper. Stiles laughed as he glimpsed the horror on the man's face a second before flames leapt from the engine.

A fire cloud rolled and blazed apart the night behind the Devil's Horsemen. Stiles kept laughing. Maybe that was the sign, he decided, that marked the beginning of a major victory. The night was going to be saved, and by sheer and insane brute force, after all.

STILES GRABBED the coke from the vault as fast as he could, pitching the bricks to his men, screaming for them to move faster. But they were hurling questions at him from all sides, their voices ripped with panic and anger. What about the others? The old ladies? What was the plan?

Stiles screamed, "No one gets near the CP. Shoot anybody who doesn't listen. Load the van, then we're gone."

He sweated, laboring with a fury to get the coke tossed into the waiting van. They were gone, history, once the van was loaded. Nothing and no one was going to stop them now.

Then he heard the familiar and terrifying bleat of rotor blades, closing, hard and fast, on his command post. Just like that, guys outside were screaming, cursing and firing their weapons.

Stiles froze, then glimpsed all the bricks still there. So much white beauty, so much money. He wanted to cry all of a sudden, but cursed instead, a long screaming oath that rang in his ears a second before the whole room shattered in a blinding light and a deafening roar.

GRIMALDI FOUND BOLAN'S directions to the biker compound, right on the money. Rearmed, the pilot came in over the trees, spotted the clearing and the dark structures below. He turned on the spotlight, raking it over a dozen figures with weapons. If there was any doubt he was on target for a clean sweep of the Devil's Horsemen it was cleared up, in no uncertain terms, a moment later.

Soaring over the compound, he saw them open up on the helicopter with autofire. A hundred yards or so west, Grimaldi saw another group of shadows by a large building. They were also firing from that direction.

Grimaldi worked the warbird so that the searchlight washed over a van near the large structure. Bearded faces were pinned in the harsh glare of white light, and the ace pilot saw they were clearly loading bricks of cocaine into a van. In a frenzy, bikers were surging in and out of the large structure, firing their weapons with one hand and hurling kilos of cocaine into the van with the other.

The Stony Man pilot grabbed the gunstick, dropped a blanket of minigun fire over the Devil's Horsemen and sent bloody and chopped up figures sprawling from the beam of light. Then he started punching buttons.

A dozen 40 mm grenades and one TOW did the job.

Grimaldi banked the aircraft away from the roaring fire that uprooted the building and incinerated the van. The Devil's Horsemen were finished. All was gone, burned up and hurled for as far as he could see. Man, machine and poison. Coke dreams, the ambitions and unrequited lust of savages, were all but vaporized in a heartbeat.

Time to link up with Bolan. He checked his watch, figuring the big guy was by now either online for the next phase or...

Grimaldi shoved that thought out of his head as he flew away from the raging inferno.

"WE'RE NOT EXACTLY certain what happened here tonight, but I can tell you, it looks like a war zone. I have never seen anything like it in my life. First reports indicate the five tractor trailers might have been transporting drugs. There's been word that cocaine, somehow, was found in the woods, or traces of the drug were—"

Tartaglia screamed at the top of his lungs, then hurled the shot glass through the giant screen TV in his living room.

"No, no, no!"

Enraged, locked in a red world of pure hate and fury, Don Paolo pulled out the Colt .45 pistol. They were sitting on the couch, his couch, in his home, still drinking his booze, smoking his cigars and taking his money. The salt-and-pepper DEA agents. They dropped their drinks and held up their hands while shrieking their innocence.

Tartaglia was gripped by murderous insanity. His world had ended. Life was over. And he didn't need to know anymore about the disaster on I-95.

It was over. The kingdom had toppled.

And if he was going down, he was taking a whole lot of people with him.

Starting with the smug but now terrified DEA turncoats.

"What are you doing?" Wilkins screamed, leaping to his feet.

"Are you fucking crazy?" Johnson bellowed. "You can't kill us, we're the law!"

"Fuck the law! Fuck you! Fuck anybody comes through my door!" Tartaglia raged, glimpsing Parker and his other so-called close associates scrambling to get out of the line of fire. Tartaglia started squeezing the trigger. They were taking .45ACP rounds through the chest and face, blood spraying everywhere. Screams and curses followed as they fell over the coffee table and smashed glass. When the initial chaos was over, Tartaglia heard something out front.

Gunfire.

The clip was dry, but Tartaglia was so locked in rage he kept squeezing the trigger.

From some great distance, it seemed, he finally heard one of his soldiers yelling something at him.

The ceaseless racket of weapons' fire on the front grounds finally penetrated Don Paolo's blind rage.

The Don heard a voice cry, "We're being hit!"

16

Bolan's van crashed the front gate of the Don's Palm Beach estate, sending two gunmen scrambling to greet the Executioner with autofire. In short, he announced the bitter end, the bloody burial for Tartaglia with a brazen show of force, letting the godfather of Miami know his reign was over.

The soldier had both the portside and starboard M-60 machine guns out on their swivel mounts, with twin flaming and sweeping streams of bullets hitting the Don's soldiers and kicking them off their feet as soon as the Executioner bulldozed through the wrought-iron barrier.

Ahead, Bolan saw two more gunmen scurry down the drive, assault rifles and SMGs chattering and barking rounds at the black war wagon. Enemy lead zinged, thudded and pounded the hull but the soldier kept on rolling, firing the M-60s by gunstick. With time working against him, the Executioner knew there was no other way than a full-frontal assault.

Up to that point, it had been a straight and hard run down the I-95 for Bolan to make the Don's oceanfront Palm Beach estate. All the soldiers, security cameras, electric fences and guard dogs in the world weren't going to save the Don now.

Still, there were many things left for Bolan to do—such as contact Tasker and have him round up Waters under a DEA protective umbrella—but it was one hit at a time. If Bolan didn't make it through the night, Waters wouldn't either. All that was left to be done was finish off the Don and his soldiers, burn down the Rodrigos and give anyone who wanted that second chance a firm hope tomorrow would come.

Bolan was locked on and driven, pumped and primed, going all the way until the narcohydra was crushed.

Bulldoze and blaze.

If it was armed and moving, the Executioner stitched it with 7.62 mm NATO projectiles.

The run up the drive was short but littered with dead Mafia soldiers. The Don's men bounded down the steps, firing on the run, but Bolan's twin flesh shredders dropped them as they ran. Blood and shredded cloth rained up the steps, between the marbled columns, watering the palms and ferns with crimson.

Bolan poured 20 mm cannonfire at a trio of hardmen throwing themselves behind some vehicles as he rounded the drive. Metal and flesh took to the air as two explosions roared through the night. A streaking and skybound figure plowed through the French double doors of the second-story landing, then appeared to bounce back and lay to eternal rest on a palm tree.

The Executioner hit the brakes, killed the engine, pocketed the keys and grabbed his Uzi submachine gun. On the drive in, he had strapped on the combat webbing, fitted now with ten frag grenades.

Grimaldi was on hold, waiting for orders.

Bolan exited the van, armed and let fly one, then another frag bomb. The lethal eggs sailed through the wide-open double front doors, detonating just as five hardmen with automatic weapons surged outside.

The twin blasts shredded the enemy, toppled them or sent them flying over the drive. From the house, weapons ceased firing as screams of agony trailed over the compound.

Uzi poised to fire in one hand, drawing the mammoth .44 Magnum Desert Eagle with the other, Bolan gave his rear and flanks a hard sweep, combat senses on full alert. Most likely, the Don had sent whatever was left of his army of soldiers, his best, most skilled, most determined and loyal killers, with the now shredded ruins of his convoy. A skeleton crew, it appeared to Bolan, was all that remained to guard the Don's crumbling empire.

It wasn't only going to crumble, it was going to topple to nothing but blood and ashes and shattered dreams of savage will and ambition.

Bolan plunged into the cordite and smoke. Scenery was shrouded by showering debris, but he was only interested in moving objects anyway. Ahead, down the foyer, he guessed, guys with hardware scrambled into position.

Time wasn't on Bolan's side, and in the next sev-

eral seconds it most certainly ran out for the hardforce, crouched at the end of the hall. The Executioner pitched two more frag bombs through the
swirling clouds, then ducked into an adjacent hall as
bullets whizzed past his head.

Someone screamed, "Grenades!"

Way too late.

A double blast of fireballs plastered chunks of
flesh to the gleaming white ceiling and walls.

Bolan surged on, Uzi stammering in one hand, the
Desert Eagle booming out .44 hollowpoint slugs in
the other hand. Three more gunners loomed up in
the soldier's deathsights, wheeling around the corner. They were greeted by lead death. Blood flew
from shattered skulls or spurted from leaking chests.
One guy was grabbing his face, wailing he was blind
when Bolan's Desert Eagle ended his suffering.

Instinctively, the soldier knew he'd be met by
fierce resistance when he reached the end of the hall.

Caution paid off.

A handgun boomed from somewhere beyond the
wafting tendrils of smoke, stone chips lashing at Bolan's face. On the run, he spotted a long white couch
and flung himself through the air.

More gunfire rained over Bolan's head while he
secured cover.

"You bastard! Whoever the fuck you are, you
ruined me! I'll fucking kill you!"

Bolan didn't have to look to know the last survivor was none other than Don Paolo. A voice of
rage, screaming curses, knifed the air.

Tartaglia was insane, holding his ground in the living room.

Lead drilled through the couch, and Bolan rolled to the floor on his knees and elbows, and crawled toward the far end of his cover. Shots kept thundering in his ears, but Tartaglia was pumping his rounds in the opposite direction.

Bolan made his move.

The Executioner popped up. The Don made eye contact with Bolan, his jaw seeming to sag in utter disbelief—or maybe acceptance of the bitter end. Whichever, Bolan would never know, nor did he care to ask.

Bolan held back on the Uzi's trigger and thundered off three .44 Magnum rounds from the Desert Eagle, both weapons recoiling in the soldier's fists. Downrange, the Don screamed, his Colt .45 firing toward the ceiling as he was driven back.

Tartaglia's chest erupted in crimson gore under the onslaught. Don Paolo was lifted off his feet and launched into a fish tank. Glass exploded, and water and flopping fish showered the Don as he plunged to marbled floor.

Long moments of utter silence followed. Bolan rolled toward Tartaglia and surveyed his surroundings. Six dead men stared up at the Executioner, sprawled around the couch or draped over the splintered ruins of a coffee table. He recognized one of the dead as the lawyer, Parker. Damn tough luck there, but every man, Bolan knew, made his own choice.

Then Bolan saw the smoking ruins of the giant

screen TV and put together what had most likely happened here.

The Don had gone berserk.

Bolan toed Tartaglia, laying among the flopping bodies of colorful fish. No response.

The king was dead.

BOLAN WALKED DOWN the steps, swiftly making his way for the war wagon.

It was strange, he thought, how the night was suddenly so still, quiet with death strewed, behind, beside and before him. Nothing moved down the drive or about the compound. No sirens or flashing lights. Yet.

Bolan hopped into the van, then raised Grimaldi. "On-line, Sarge?"

Bolan filled Grimaldi in. The ace pilot, he found out, had put the torch to the Devil's Horsemen, buried what was left of the bikers and put his own personal touch with his copter on their own dreams and evil ambitions.

The Executioner was told Grimaldi's ETA to the Rodrigo estate was ten minutes. Bolan asked him to stretch it some, to give him a little time to get down the road.

Signing off, the soldier drove out the front gates of Don Paolo's shattered kingdom.

BOLAN HIT THE RODRIGO compound with van in the same bulldoze manner as he had Don Paolo's.

Only this time he had a little help from his friend.

Death from above fell over the place as Bolan gave Grimaldi the green light.

Hardmen were scrambling everywhere, running down the drive, surging outside the mansion.

Together with his air fire support, Bolan unloaded on the enemy with everything he had left in his arsenal.

The black gunship hovered over the circular drive, minigun blazing, mowing down the Rodrigo's hardforce.

Twin M-60s blazed from the van as Bolan dropped any and everything that was armed and running. On the move, he came around the drive, pounding out relentless 20 mm cannonfire.

"Hit it, second story and the front door, G-Force," Bolan ordered Grimaldi.

The Executioner hit the brakes. With a fresh clip in his Uzi, the soldier watched, forced to wait a few seconds as Grimaldi dumped rockets on the mansion. Tremendous explosions thundered the night.

The entire second story of the mansion was blasted into the air.

"Get ready to pick me up next time you see me, G-Force. I'm going in. Take it as far as everything on your end is holding. We look able to fly, untouched?"

"That's affirmative."

"Do a sweep of the compound. Burn anything down if it walks and is armed."

It was all Grimaldi needed to know, and what the pilot had told Bolan was all he needed to hear. No air traffic was tracking Grimaldi. All radio frequencies were jammed. But either way, Bolan had to move fast.

It was another frontal assault, pitching armed frag grenades through the swirling wall of smoke. Shadowy figures charged, right into the twin fireballs and lethal bits of steel shrapnel Bolan had thrown at their rush.

Inside, the Executioner was again ready for the enemy to greet him with deadly intent. He wasn't disappointed. From several directions gunmen scurried toward him, firing their assault rifles and SMGs on the fly. Another frag grenade took care of the hardforce, shredding their numbers and blasting them across the living room.

Smoke and cordite filled Bolan's senses. Somewhere outside the compound he heard the bleat of rotors, then made out the chatter of minigun fire. Distant screams knifed the air. Grimaldi was hard at work, mopping up.

Two figures emerged from a hallway. One man had a ponytail, the other shadow, beyond the falling debris whirling toward Bolan, had angry dark eyes and a mustache. The soldier had seen both men in DEA intelligence photos.

Bolan had the Rodrigos, lined up with his Uzi subgun.

Both brothers cut loose with handguns.

The ceiling groaned above Bolan as sections of the roof caved and descended near the brothers.

The Executioner held back on the Uzi's trigger, emptying the whole clip into the brothers. Even as their bodies twitched and ruptured under the soldier's lead burial, they screamed, cursed and died every bit as hard and angry as Don Paolo.

They dropped, one brother falling on top of the other.

A quick search of the carnage heaped and strewed around the living room and Bolan was satisfied they were finished for good here.

Outside, he spotted several armed figures, piling into a Cadillac. The wheelman fired up the engine, and a gunman poked out the back window, then opened up with a submachine gun. Reaching cover behind a Jaguar, Bolan drew his Desert Eagle. He was about to pull the trigger when Grimaldi soared from the far north end of the compound and spotted the trouble area.

The Cadillac was racing the front gate when the helicopter swooped down and blew the vehicle off the driveway with a few well-placed 40 mm grenades.

Moments later, the aircraft landed near the flaming ruins of its last assault.

Bolan bounded through the side door and joined Grimaldi in the cockpit. One loose end remained— Sal Tartaglia. But by all accounts, the mobster was on his death bed and certainly in no shape to take over what remained of The Family. Sal was one mafioso who would get to die in bed.

"Let's go home, Jack," the Executioner said. "We're finished here."

Take
2 explosive books
plus a
mystery bonus
FREE

James Axler

OUTLANDERS™

OUTER DARKNESS

Kane and his companions are transported to an alternate reality where the global conflagration didn't happen—and humanity had expelled the Archons from the planet. Things are not as rosy as they may seem, as the Archons return for a final confrontation....

Book #3 in the new Lost Earth Saga, a trilogy that chronicles our heroes' paths through three very different alternative realities...where the struggle against the evil Archons goes on....

Shadow THE EXECUTIONER®
as he battles evil for 352 pages of
heart-stopping action!

SuperBolan®

#61452	DAY OF THE VULTURE	$5.50 U.S. $6.50 CAN.	☐ ☐
#61453	FLAMES OF WRATH	$5.50 U.S. $6.50 CAN.	☐ ☐
#61454	HIGH AGGRESSION	$5.50 U.S. $6.50 CAN.	☐ ☐
#61455	CODE OF BUSHIDO	$5.50 U.S. $6.50 CAN.	☐ ☐
#61456	TERROR SPIN	$5.50 U.S. $6.50 CAN.	☐ ☐

(limited quantities available on certain titles)

TOTAL AMOUNT	$
POSTAGE & HANDLING	$
($1.00 for one book, 50¢ for each additional)	
APPLICABLE TAXES*	$ _____
TOTAL PAYABLE	$ _____
(check or money order—please do not send cash)	

To order, complete this form and send it, along with a check or money order for the total above, payable to Gold Eagle Books, to: **In the U.S.:** 3010 Walden Avenue, P.O. Box 9077, Buffalo, NY 14269-9077; **In Canada:** P.O. Box 636, Fort Erie, Ontario, L2A 5X3.

Name: _____

Address: _____ City: _____

State/Prov.: _____ Zip/Postal Code: _____

*New York residents remit applicable sales taxes.
Canadian residents remit applicable GST and provincial taxes.

GSBBACK1